The Flip Side

P E T E R S

F R A S E R

&

D U N L O P

503/4 THE CHAMBERS
CHELSEA HARBOUR
LONDON SW10 0XF

AGENT:
ROYALTY SHEET Nº:
PUBLICATION DATE:
CATEGORY:

Also by Andrew Matthews

Stiks and Stoans

For younger readers

Family Stuff
Loads of Trouble
Dr Monsoon Taggert's Amazing Finishing Academy

The Flip Side

ANDREW MATTHEWS

mammoth

First published in Great Britain in 2001 by Mammoth
an imprint of Egmont Children's Books Limited
a division of Egmont Holding Limited
239 Kensington High Street, London, W8 6SA

ISBN 0 7497 4258 5

10 9 8 7 6 5 4 3 2 1

A CIP catalogue record for this book is available at the British Library

Typeset by Avon Dataset Ltd, Bidford on Avon, B50 4JH
Printed in Great Britain by Cox & Wyman Ltd, Reading, Berkshire

for Rosemary, with love

Contents

All the world's a stage,

And all the men and women merely players.

They have their exits and their entrances,

And one man in his time plays many parts,

His acts being seven ages. At first the infant,

Mewling and puking in the nurse's arms.

And then the whining schoolboy, with his satchel

And shining morning face, creeping like a snail

Unwillingly to school. And then the lover,

Sighing like furnace, with a woful ballad

Made to his mistress' eyebrow. Then, a soldier,

Full of strange oaths, and bearded like the pard,

Jealous in honour, sudden and quick in quarrel,

Seeking the bubble reputation

Even in the cannon's mouth. And then the justice,

In fair round belly with good capon lined,

With eyes severe and beard of formal cut,

Full of wise saws and modern instances;

And so he plays his part. The sixth age shifts

Into the lean and slippered pantaloon,

With spectacles on nose and pouch on side,

His youthful hose well saved, a world too wide

For his shrunk shank, and his big, manly voice,

Turning again toward childish treble, pipes

And whistles in his sound. Last scene of all,

That ends this strange, eventful history,

Is second childishness and mere oblivion,

Sans teeth, sans eyes, sans taste, sans everything.

William Shakespeare, *As You Like It*, Act II, Scene vii

1

Entrances

Life's really weird, you know? You have to live it forwards, but it only makes sense when you look back on it, and even then you can't be certain exactly why you did what you did. You might have been influenced by all kinds of things: the weather, dreams, genes, hormones, other people. The trickiest part is working out who you were at the time, and I'm here to tell you that the more you analyse yourself, the more you're not there.

OK, I know what you're thinking – *This guy must be some kind of psycho*! – right?

Wrong.

Let me give you a for instance. Say you're mucking about in school one lunchtime, and a window gets broken, and you're caught. Imagine you're explaining to a teacher what happened. Now you go home and tell your parents about it. You don't talk to them in the same way, do you? Later on, one of your best mates drops by and you give them Version Three, using words you wouldn't *dare* use to your parents or to a teacher. Each time, you're a slightly different person.

So which one is you?

In fact there's a whole load of different people inside you, like a collection of masks. You change your mask according to the situation you find yourself in. Sorting out which one is really you is practically impossible, because the person it's hardest to be honest with is yourself. And here's the spooky bit: maybe when you take all the masks off you're not anybody; maybe you're as blank as the white stuff inside a Pritt stick.

I'm writing this because I'm sorted now, but I lost it for a while and I want to understand why. To do it properly I have to put in everything – daydreams, fantasies, nightmares, the lot – or it won't be real. Actually, it wasn't real, that's the whole point; but the way it was unreal was pretty awesome.

The only reason I'm willing to tell you about it is that you don't know me. This is like getting online with someone in Australia: you can tell them things about yourself that you wouldn't tell anybody else, because they can't spread them around to anyone who matters. In fact, if you like, you can make out that you're the person you'd *like* to be, instead of the person you are. This isn't lying, exactly – more like a game of let's pretend – but it's not exactly telling the truth either.

Of course I could be doing that – pretending that all this happened to me when it didn't. You'll never know and it doesn't matter. Reality is like beauty and ugliness, it all depends on how you look at things, and how you look at things depends on the person you are.

Whoever that might be.

2

The whining schoolboy

It was sunset, one of those blazing red jobs with magenta clouds that were orange underneath. I was riding a black stallion along a beach. The tide was out and the beach was deserted, miles of white sand curving out to a rocky headland. The wind was whipping through my hair and whistling in my ears. I was totally free – no stress, no hang-ups, nowhere I had to be, nothing else I ought to be doing – and it was brilliant . . .

Then the alarm-clock woke me up.

The feeling of freedom went – ZAPPO! – and I was me again: fifteen, in Year Ten, with a load of GCSE coursework like you wouldn't believe. It was the start of another thrill-packed schoolday and I had French first lesson. What kind of sadist designs a timetable that has French for first lesson? Most kids are still having trouble speaking English at that time of the morning.

So, did I leap out of bed, do twenty press-ups, look at myself in the wardrobe mirror and say, 'Every day, in every way, I'm getting better and better,' or did I pull the duvet over my head to try to get back to the beach?

Guess.

Eventually Dad shouted up the stairs, 'Robert, it's nearly half past! Shift yourself!'

This is what he always shouts; at least it's better

than 'Rise and shine!'

Twenty minutes later I was showered, dressed, downstairs and raring to crawl back into bed.

Dad was mixing American biscuits – you know, the ones that are like scones with no sugar in? He was wearing a butcher's apron, and the bits of dough stuck to his hands made him look as though he had a skin disease.

I went to the fridge, grabbed the orange juice and I was just raising it to my lips when Dad said, 'Don't even think of drinking it straight from the carton. Get a glass.'

'Mum up?'

'She left early. She has a meeting in London at nine. A Dutch company wants to . . .'

I turned off my ears. I didn't want to know all the details, and neither do you. It goes: Mum runs a software-design business, Dad is one of her employees. Mum swans off all over the place wheeler-dealing, Dad mainly works from home.

They're supposed to split the housework between them, but Dad cops most of it – like, my old man is a New Man.

When Dad had been through it down to the last megabyte, I said, 'Sounds good!'

Dad was rolling out dough by this time. He said, 'Anything you need?'

'A passionate affair, a million pounds and a life would be nice.'

Dad sighed. He has this way of sighing that says, 'Communicating with other people is incredibly time-consuming and tedious and I wish, just once, that I could be given a straightforward answer.' Which is pretty good for a sigh, you have to admit.

'I meant that I have to go shopping this morning, so is there anything that you'd like me to get?'

'I could use some mouthwash – but don't buy that blue stuff again, it sucks. I prefer the regular brand.'

Dad gave me a look. 'Sucks? Regular? Are you turning into an American, Robert?'

'I'm just your regular teenager, Pops,' I said. 'Blame the media and peer pressure.'

Kev called for me at eight twenty and we walked to school. When we were younger we used to go by bus, but then we sussed that travelling to school by bus was too fast: walking gives you more of a chance to psych yourself up.

Kev had tried to hide his uniform by putting on a hooded jacket over his school jumper, but the regulation charcoal-grey trousers with turn-ups and sensible black shoes gave him away.

He said, 'Hear that story on the news this morning?'

'Which story?'

'This bloke wanted a number plate to match his initials? Then he found out it was cheaper to change his name by deed poll so his initials matched the

number plate he already had. He saved himself two
K. Cool!'

'It all depends.'

'On what?'

'The letters on his number plate.'

'Huh?'

'Try it yourself,' I said. 'Make up a name for the
number plate of the next car we pass.'

We walked past a blue Renault – ACF.

'Alexander Charles Foster,' said Kev. 'Easy!'

'How about that one, KRD?'

'Kevin Robert Davies.'

The next number plate was HTX. Kev frowned,
scratched his head and went, 'E-e-r . . .!'

I said, 'Harrison T. Xylophone.'

'What does the T stand for?'

'Nothing. Just sounds good.'

'That's cheating, Rob!'

'How can it be cheating when it's my game? I
make the rules. No points for boring names. The

weirder the name, the bigger the score.'

Kev held up his hand for a high five, then said, 'You're on! Loser buys the doughnuts at break.'

As we neared the next car there was actually a spark of tension between us – like that's how sad our lives were.

BHT

Kev said, 'Bertram Hieronymous Talbot.'

'Four out of ten. Beauregard Hedge-Trimmer.'

We both cackled. I don't suppose anybody else on earth would have found it funny but – hey, that's Kev and I for you.

I said, 'Is that a new jacket?'

'Uh-huh.'

'It's, er, bright, isn't it?'

Kev shrugged. 'Haven't you heard? Canary yellow is the new black.'

'Kev, ever heard the term *fashion victim*?'

'Yes. Have you heard the term *loser geek with no sense of style whatsoever*?'

'What d'you mean, no sense of style whatsoever?'

'D'you have mirrors in your house?'

'Sure.'

'Take a look in one sometime.'

I ignored him. I thought he was just being ratty because he'd lost the number plate game.

Last lesson was English with Mrs Porter, or as I preferred to think of it, English with Milena. Milena Griffin's mother was Czech, which accounted for Milena's olive skin, jet-black hair and dark, almond-shaped eyes. I hadn't noticed Milena until the start of Year Ten, but once I had, I couldn't stop. She fascinated me. Her eyebrows were black rainbows, her teeth were like . . . well, teeth – but perfect. Her smile made my day: not that she'd ever smiled at me and not that she was ever likely to. Milena was intelligent, sensitive, sweet, shy, gorgeous, wasn't going out with anybody and didn't know that I existed.

Mrs Porter said, 'Right – *As You Like It*. What did you all make of Act Four, Scene One?'

Not a lot, by the initial reaction.

Gary Middleton raised his hand and the rest of the class groaned because Gary fancied himself as a Lad.

'Yes, Gary?' said Mrs Porter.

'I reckon Shakespeare must have been some sort of perv, Miss.'

'What makes you think that?'

'Well, he's got this girl making out she's a boy making out he's a girl. That's a bit iffy, isn't it?'

Jane Wallace piped up from the back, 'Shakespeare is using this scene to play with the concept of gender stereotyping.'

'Yeah?' said Gary. 'That's not all he was playing with, if you ask me!'

You had to laugh at Gary, like you sometimes have to laugh at a tabloid headline because it's so crass.

When the laughter died down, Mrs Porter said, 'It's more complicated than you think, Gary. You see, in Shakespeare's time it was considered indecent for women to appear on the stage. All the female roles were taken by young boys. So in this scene you would have had a boy pretending to be a girl who's pretending to be a boy pretending to be a girl.'

Gary's face did peculiar things as he tried to get his head round the idea, then he said, 'Ugh, that's gross!'

Some of the other guys in the group grunted to show that they agreed with Gary, but I didn't. The idea of a boy being a girl being a boy being a girl didn't put me off; in fact, I found it intriguing.

And that, though I didn't know it at the time, was when it all started.

When I got home I heard the clatter of a computer keyboard coming from Dad's study and figured he was hard at it. I did an hour's coursework, which I reckoned entitled me to a break, so I went to check out what was on TV. I channel-hopped into the middle of one of those American chat shows where the hostess gets people to say incredibly personal things about themselves in front of millions of viewers. Only this edition of the show wasn't like that, and I got hooked.

Lined up in front of the studio audience were eight glamorous babes. And I'm talking *American* glamorous here – spangly tight sheath-dresses, shoes with heels you could use as weapons, fake-fur stoles, false eyelashes and loads of lavishly applied make-up. They all looked like women, but the point of the show was that some of them were men and the audience had to guess who was what.

Most of them were obvious – I could tell the men from the way they walked or their voices – but I had no idea about Number Eight and it was disturbing because he/she was pretty horny in a blatant sort of way.

Number Seven ripped off his wig to reveal his true identity and said, 'Listen, all you guys out there! Get dressed in drag at least once in your lives, because it feels fabulous!'

At this point my viewing was interrupted by Dad, who wandered into the room, glanced at the TV and said, 'What *is* this?'

'The Ricky Williams Show.'

'Who are those people?'

'Some are real women, some are blokes dressed up as women.'

'And they broadcast it at a time when children might be watching? Unbelievable!'

Dad sounded shocked and disgusted, and I wondered what was bugging him so much.

Talking to Dad made me miss finding out whether Number Eight was a he or a she, but I was glad. If it had been a man, I would've had to be confused about getting turned on by him, and if it had been a woman I would have been . . . well, disappointed, I suppose.

Funny how the *really* exciting things are always the ones that are most different, isn't it?

I was right about Dad being bugged by The Ricky Williams Show. He sounded off to Mum about it over dinner.

As she listened to him, Mum lost her tired look and went from hard-nosed career woman to Mum.

Dad said, 'I've never seen anything so decadent in my life! What kind of message would it have given to impressionable young minds? It was completely unnatural.'

Mum cracked up and almost fell off her chair.

Dad looked at her. 'What?'

'You. We wear artificial fabrics and we live in a centrally-heated house, surrounded by a society that spends most of its time staring at images on an electronic screen. The whole world is unnatural!'

'No it isn't.'

'The human world is,' said Mum.

And you know what? She was absolutely right.

3

All the world's a stage

Shakespeare, The Ricky Williams Show and Mum started me thinking about things I'd never really thought about before: like girls and boys, what was natural and what was unnatural. I'd taken a lot of stuff for granted, because I thought it was the way things ought to be. Girls were in a box labelled:

dolls, make-up, hairdos, giggling, gossip; the label on the boys' box said: *rough, loud, dirty jokes, football*. Meanwhile, something else was going on underneath – tomboys, nancy-boys, boy–girls and girl–boys, like that old Blur song. At my infants school there had been girls who played football and flattened anyone who tried to tackle them, and boys who'd cried easily. Female executives wore trouser suits and there were male showbiz personalities who earned their living by impersonating women. A young woman who'd once been a young man had won the Eurovision Song Contest – so what was natural any more, and in the case of the Eurovision Song Contest, what had ever been? Nothing was as cut and dried as I'd assumed, and when had I begun assuming?

Like, if you go to a pantomime when you're little, you aren't freaked that the principal boy is a female and the dame is a man in drag, you accept it as part of the fun. At what point do you stop thinking it's fun, and why? What makes gender such a serious issue and how come guys are so sensitive about it? I mean, girls hug and kiss when they say hello and goodbye, but guys don't. Why not? – is there something they're scared of?

On the way to school with Kev, I had questions whirling round me like a flock of roosting starlings.

Kev said, 'Michael Motorised-Orange!'

'Huh?'

'That number plate – MMO. Michael Motorised-Orange.'

I smiled out of politeness. 'Kev, how would you feel if a girl said she fancied you?'

'I'd admire her good taste.'

'How about a guy?'

Kev gave me a hard stare. 'You what?'

'If a guy said he fancied you, it'd be just as flattering as if a girl said it, wouldn't it?'

Kev went pink, uncomfortable and defensive. 'How would I know? Most people find the idea of a guy and another guy a bit . . . you know.'

'But say you and this other guy were ship-wrecked on a desert island, and then one night you were both feeling really horny, would you . . .?'

'I'd rather use a couple of coconuts,' said Kev.

He was trying to turn it into a joke; I wouldn't let him. 'D'you think it's a turn-off for a gay guy if he finds out that a girl fancies him, or is he, like, curious?'

Kev was bright red by now. 'Rob, can we change the subject? This is starting to do my head in!'

We dropped it after that, but I thought that Kev's reaction had been typical: sexuality was private and personal, but at the same time it mattered what other people thought about it. You had to think about sex in a straight line – yeah, *straight*, right? Like as in: heterosexual; no straying from the footpath; no experimentation. But the world was full of possibilities, and if you couldn't try them out, why were they there?

* * *

In English, Mrs Porter got us to move the tables and chairs back to create a space in the centre of the room. She said, 'Since *As You Like It*, Act Four, Scene One provoked such a lively debate yesterday, I thought it would be illuminating to perform part of it. After all, Shakespeare didn't intend people to read his plays, he wanted audiences to see them acted in a theatre. I need two volunteers. Milena, you've just volunteered to be Rosalind, and Robert has just volunteered to be Orlando.'

I said, 'Me, Miss?'

'Is there anyone else called Robert in this group?'

Did I detect a glint of mischief in Mrs Porter's eyes, like, had she picked us deliberately because she knew I had a thing about Milena? I couldn't tell, and anyway I had other things on my mind – like the blush that was going all the way from my navel to the top of my head.

Mrs Porter said, 'Remember, Milena, you're teasing Orlando. Robert, try to act lovesick.'

'I'll give it my best shot, Miss.'

'Take it from *My fair Rosalind*'.

Right from the off, Milena was incredible. For a girl who was usually so shy, she had a surprisingly detailed knowledge of Advanced Flirting. She flicked her hair, tilted her head to look up at me through her lashes, flounced, pouted and generally gave me a hard time.

I started by just reading the lines, but I gradually got into it and lost myself in being someone else.

At the end the class applauded; not all of the applause was ironic.

Mrs Porter said, 'Well done, you two! Does anyone have any suggestions as to how we could have made that scene more effective?'

Someone said, 'Costume.'

Someone else said, 'Lighting.'

And then everybody wanted a say. Mrs Porter

held up her hand for quiet. 'One at a time, please! Gary?'

Gary had this big grin. 'If Shakespeare's mucking about with stereotypes in this scene, I reckon we should go for it!'

'How?'

'Get them to switch over; Milena should be Orlando and Robert should be Rosalind.'

There was a lot of shocked blinking at this, because Gary Middleton had come up with an original idea.

And then Jane Wallace, Little Miss Intellectual, said, 'Put Milena in trousers and Robert in a dress.'

I said, 'Hold on a min–!' But I could tell from the faces all round me that my objection would be overruled. I was fated, doomed; I was never going to live it down; I was going to be Robert Hunt, Frock Boy. The idea made chills run down my spine but there was another feeling too, a little flicker of something that I didn't recognise. I put it down to stage fright.

I told Kev about the English lesson as we walked home.

He said, 'You and Milena? Was it a love scene?'

'Kind of.'

'How did it go?'

'Fine. We're going to do the scene again next lesson, but on the stage this time. Mrs Porter's booked the main hall. It should be quite interesting.'

'Shakespeare, interesting? Why?'

As casually as possible, I said, 'Oh, I have to wear a dress.'

'A *dress*?'

'Yeah. The scene is about swapping roles, so Milena and I are swapping.'

'And you said yes?'

'Uh-huh.'

'Let me make sure I've got this straight.

Tomorrow, you're going to ponce about on stage, in front of people, *wearing a dress*?'

'It's just acting, Kev. Theatre is all about illusion.'

I didn't know whether I was trying to convince Kev or myself.

Kev made a noise that indicated disgust, like a BLEUCH! and said, 'You'd never get me into one of those things, mate!'

'What, a Shakespeare play?'

'No, a dress!'

I said, 'I don't know, Kev. A little pink cocktail dress would bring out the colour of your eyes.'

'Get lost!' said Kev. He sounded genuinely angry.

'I'm joking! You know, jokes – those things you laugh at?'

'Only when they're funny, Rob.'

4

Enter Rosalind

Next day was Friday, the last day before the Easter break. I woke up feeling that I had something to look forward to, and it was more than the holiday, it was the performance on stage with Milena. We were going to be together – and sure, it was only acting, but it was a start. Maybe she'd see me differently afterwards, come up to me and say, 'Hey, Robert! You and I are pretty good together, what say we go out one evening?'

Maybe it would be just like I knew it was never going to be.

When I got downstairs I was granted the rare privilege of seeing my mother at breakfast-time. She was in the lounge, wearing a black suit, drinking coffee and frowning at an e-mail hard copy. Dad was in the kitchen, fussing over a saucepan of scrambled eggs; he was wearing his butcher's apron and a frazzled look.

'Bad news?' I asked Mum.

'Yes and no. The company I met on Wednesday wants me to work with them on a project.'

'So that's good?'

'Yes, but it means I'll have to spend next week in Amsterdam. I wanted to take a few days off so we could . . .'

'Play happy families?'

'Spend some time together – the three of us. I don't see you as much as I ought to. Sometimes I feel I'm neglecting you and your father. I think he deserves a break.'

'Yeah,' I said. 'Have you noticed how he's started to let himself go recently? I mean – that hair!'

'You shouldn't make fun of him, Robert. He works hard. Not many men would be prepared to give me the kind of support he does. Perhaps the two of you could do something together over Easter.'

'What, like the male bonding thing – hunt grizzlies in the forest?'

'You could go for a long walk in the country.'

'I'm not too fussed about the country, it's full of midges and animal droppings. I think Dad would probably prefer to go to a kitchen shop and check out feather dusters.'

Mum sighed. 'That's what I mean! He needs taking out of himself.'

Flash of inspiration! I said, 'Why doesn't he go to Amsterdam with you? He could visit one of those coffee shops and get off his face – that would take him out of himself.'

'I don't know about the coffee shop, but taking him to Amsterdam isn't a bad idea. We could all go.'

'Wouldn't it be better if it was just you and Dad? I hear that three's a crowd.'

'But what about you?'

'I'll be fine here. I can throw a party and have my friends trash the place.'

Mum frowned. 'Isn't it illegal to leave you on your own before you're sixteen?'

'Only if someone finds out. I won't tell if you won't.'

'I'm not sure . . .'

It was time for a little manipulation, so I pulled an offended face and said, 'Don't you trust me?'

'Of course I do.'

'Then take Dad to Amsterdam. I'm sixteen in August – what difference does a few months make? Live dangerously while you're still young enough to enjoy it.'

Mum narrowed her eyes. 'If I didn't know better, I'd say that you were trying to get rid of us.'

I said, 'Sure am!'

Mum laughed because she thought I was joking. I had her halfway convinced about Amsterdam, but I knew that Dad wasn't going to be so easy.

English was lesson two. Mrs Porter sat the rest of the group in the well of the hall and took Milena and me into what she called 'the greenroom', so we could raid the Drama department's costume collection. Before you get too impressed, I should explain that the costume collection is housed in an old cupboard and two tatty cardboard boxes.

Mrs Porter said, 'That.'

I said, 'What – *that*?'

That was a creased, full-length, green velvet dress with a gaping side seam and button-fastenings without buttons at the back.

'It looks your size. Put it on.'

'But . . . !'

'No time for buts, Robert!'

I slipped the dress over my head, pulled it down and looked in the mirror inside the cupboard door. I'd been growing my hair, going for a Kurt Cobain, retro-grunge sort of thing – sad! – and it was nearly to my shoulders. I mussed it up, pressed my lips tight together so they'd go red and did a twirl. It would have been nice if the dress had flowed with me, but it didn't; the grey trousers and black boots sticking out from under the hem didn't help either, but the total effect wasn't too bad – I hoped.

I turned around and saw that Milena had scraped her hair back in a way that made her boyish and emphasised her cheekbones at the same time. She looked great in jeans, but then Milena would have looked great in a bin-liner. She smiled at me and something went soft in her eyes as she said, 'Good day and happiness, dear Rosalind.'

I huffed and turned up my nose, because in the scene we were about to do, Rosalind was supposed to be offended with Orlando for being late.

Mrs Porter said, 'All set? Break a leg, darlings!'

Naturally, when I marched on stage wearing a dress, I was greeted with laughter and phony wolf whistles, but I thought – Stuff 'em! I'm not me, I'm Rosalind – and tried to walk the way girls who took dancing lessons walked: shoulders back, head held straight. The book was a problem; I wished that I'd memorised the lines so that I didn't have to carry it around, but when Milena made her entrance I forgot about anything else.

She was all adolescent male: awkward, testosterone-clumsy. We started the scene and suddenly it made sense. Orlando is supposed to believe that Rosalind is a boy called Ganymede, who's *pretending* to be Rosalind, but Ganymede pretends so well that Orlando starts to fall in love with him – her!

And all of a sudden I felt something leap from my subconscious mind and take over, and Rosalind was me. Robert went missing in action and left Rosalind in charge, and boy, did she ever enjoy herself! The dress had unlocked her and she made the most of her freedom. It wasn't enough for her to twist Orlando into a pretzel round her little finger, she flirted with the audience as well. Rosalind was confident, feisty, sharp-tongued – everything that Robert wasn't.

Part of me was thinking – What's got into you, Rob? – but the real question was what had got out?

At the end of the scene there was this really weird silence. I glanced down into the well of the hall and saw two rows of gobsmacked teenagers and a bemused-looking teacher. They didn't know what had hit them, and neither did I.

Eventually Mrs Porter said, 'I rather think that Milena and Robert have earned a round of applause, don't you?'

We got one and we ducked off stage into the greenroom while it was still going on. All our nervous tension turned into laughter and we leaned close to each other: hey, almost a hug!

Milena said, 'I had no idea that you could act like that. You were terrific!'

'*Rosalind* was terrific. You were pretty terrific yourself.'

Milena swept me a bow. 'Why thanks, fair Rosalind.'

I tugged at the dress. 'How do you manage in these things? It's like having your ankles tied together.'

'You think that dress is bad news? You ought to try high heels.'

Our laughter turned back into nervous tension.

Milena said, 'W-e-l-l! Better get changed.'

She sounded reluctant about it; she turned away, and in my mind Rosalind said, 'Now, you jerk! Act!'

I said, 'Are you, er, going away over Easter?'

'No. Why?'

'I just thought that if you were around, we might, kind of, you know, sort of . . .'

'Go out somewhere?'

'Mm.'

'Like, on a date?'

I said, 'Oh, sure, yeah, like as if you'd be interested – dumb, hey? I'm sorry. I must have got carried away with the play and everything. I didn't mean to . . .'

Milena said, 'Yes.'

'Huh?'

'Yes, I'll go out with you. Look me up in the phone book and give me a call.'

I thought – ?? – and – !!!

I swear that if I hadn't been wearing the dress, I wouldn't have had the nerve.

* * *

At lunchtime, Kev and I parked ourselves on the low wall near the gym and had a conversation that was more like a monologue. I was full of myself and Milena.

'It was unreal! It was like she'd known all along that I wanted to ask her out. She must be able to read my mind. You think that's possible – that two people can be so tuned into each other that they share the same thoughts?'

'Mm.'

'Freaky! You reckon anyone can do it, or does it only happen when something's, you know, special?'

'Mm.'

I stopped babbling just long enough to notice that Kev wasn't OK. He was closed in, staring at his hands without seeing them.

'Kev?'

He looked up and gave me a fake smile that came and went in a blink. 'So, it's Rob and Milena, huh? How long have you had a thing about her now?'

'Twenty-two weeks, six days and fourteen hours. What's up?'

'Nothing – absolutely nothing.'

'Come on, Kev. We know each other too well for you to hold out on me.'

'Nah, I'm just being stupid.'

'Being stupid never bothered you before.'

Kev started wriggling his shoulders as if he had an itchy back. 'It's just – well, I thought you and I would be hanging out this Easter, like we usually do. But if you and Milena are an item, I don't suppose you'll have the time.'

'What? Of course we're going to hang out to-gether, Kev. I'm going on a date, not getting married. Maybe Milena won't even like me when she gets to know me.'

'Maybe,' said Kev, not sounding convinced.

'Get a grip, will you? Girls may come and

girls may go, but mates are forever.'

I waited for Kev to make a crack, but instead he said, 'You mean that?'

'Absolutely!'

'We're always going to be friends?'

'Sure!'

'No matter what?'

'Kev, what could possibly happen to stop us being mates?'

'People change.'

I was: SYSTEMS FAILURE – RESTART! Kev was being serious and I had trouble getting my head around it because Kev and I always made jokes when we were being serious. This time Kev was *seriously* serious.

'Kev, you feeling left out or something?'

'When did I ever not feel left out?'

We'd come to the border of the Kev I thought I knew, and for the first time I realised that there was unexplored territory beyond it. I left myself a mental note: *Get together with Kev this holiday, have a laugh, put things right.*

It didn't occur to me that if I had to put things right, something must be wrong.

Dad was in the lounge, working on the laptop. He didn't look up when I said hello, but just as I was about to leave him to it, he said, 'How was today?'

I screened the version of my life where I said, 'I asked this girl out and she said yes. Oh, and by the way, I found out that wearing women's clothes really gets me off!' but it ended with Dad being given oxygen by paramedics, so I said, 'OK. You?'

'Don't ask. Your mother's badgering me into going to Amsterdam with her. Any idea why?'

'She wants to have her wicked way with you?'

Dad swore at something on the monitor and tapped the delete key. 'Of course, if I go, you'll have to come as well.'

'Why?'

Dad looked at me as if I was being really thick. 'How would you feed yourself? Who'd keep the house tidy?'

'Out of the freezer, and me. I'm not a total disaster area, Dad! I can use a microwave and a hoover. I might not use them very often, but I know how to.'

'Hah!'

I said, 'Face it, you need a break.'

'From what?'

'Yourself. Do you want me hanging round your neck for the rest of your life, or do you want me to start learning how to be independent?'

Dad went gloopy-eyed on me. 'Listen to you! You know, the first time I held you after you were born, you fitted in . . .'

'Don't go there! I might regress and throw up. I was a *baby* then, Dad. I wipe my own bottom these days. Go with Mum, have a good time. Phone me every day if you like, but trust me and give me some space, will you?'

Dad said, 'Amsterdam! The Van Gogh Museum, the Rembrandts – I can't pretend that I'm not tempted.'

'Then give in! Think of all that Edam. You'll get to use Euros, just like a real European. Everybody speaks English and the trains run on time – you'll love it!'

Dad came out of his dream. 'No, it's out of the question!'

And I knew that I'd got him.

So did Mum: when she came home she told Dad that she'd booked his flight and a double room at the Amsterdam Hilton.

Dad took a handkerchief out of his pocket and waved it like a white flag.

5

**O, how full of briers is
this working-day world!**

*The trees were all around; big redwoods, like pillars
holding up the ceiling of a cathedral, silent in their own
shadows. I could feel them watching as I struggled through
thick undergrowth. Shrubs whipped branches across my
face; brambles stretched out suckers, hooking their thorns
into my clothes to hold me back; roots pushed up out of*

the earth to trip me. There was somewhere I had to find, but there was no path to guide me; no one had ever been here before.

I broke through and staggered into a clearing that I knew was a secret place, the heart of something. In front of me was a heap of boulders. Water ran out of the gaps between the stones and formed a pool at their feet. My hands were scratched and hot. I wanted to cool them in the water of the pool, so I hunkered down at its edge.

A swaying reflection gazed up at me: a girl with anxious eyes and a vulnerable mouth. A ghost had haunted her, trapped her in the pool, with a spell that could only be broken by the right person. I reached out a hand and so did she. My fingertips brushed the water and felt warm, smooth skin.

'Rosalind,' I said.

Her hand merged with mine, her shoulder became my shoulder, her face, my face. I drew the reflection up out of the pool and left the surface blank.

* * *

Dreams: spooky! You spend a significant fraction of your life dreaming, but you can't map the Dream Place because in each dream you have you're different: sometimes you, sometimes a person you don't recognise. I don't know if dreams mean anything. Most people seem to believe they do, only when they try to describe their dreams, they find that words won't reach where the dreams came from. You can forget a dream as soon as you wake, or it can stay with you for years, like it was something that actually happened to you.

Dreams freaked me when I was a kid. I didn't know where I went when I was asleep. I'd lie in bed, fighting to stay awake. Eventually the dream would take me away, but it would always get me back by morning.

This is the kind of stuff I think about instead of watching TV. What you see on TV is other people's dreams, happening over there on a glass screen; your own dreams happen from the inside outwards.

* * *

Saturday: the start of the holiday and the first chance for a lie-in, so natch I woke up at six and couldn't get back to sleep. For want of something better to do, I grabbed *As You Like It* from the bedside unit, read Act Four, Scene One again, then turned back to the start and began reading through the whole thing. I saw it as a movie in my head:

As You Like It, *or* What You Will

starring

Milena Griffin as Orlando

Robert Hunt as Rosalind

Produced and directed by Robert Hunt

I was gone; I kept on reading as I got out of bed, went downstairs and made myself a cup of coffee that I forgot to drink. I was still reading when Dad came into the kitchen.

He said, 'Must be good.'

'Hmm.'

'What is it – Stephen King?'

'Shakespeare.'

'*Shakespeare*?'

Dad sounded alarmed; I came out of the play and saw that he *looked* alarmed. He said, 'You do realise that if you carry on like this, you run the risk of being cultured?'

'Top joke, Dad.'

'What next – Classic FM, Fine Art?'

'Please, no more! You're so funny that it hurts.'

Dad rubbed his hands together. 'Right, if I'm going to Amsterdam tomorrow, I'd better get cracking. Let's see ... washing, ironing, packing – oh, and I must remember to write you out a list of emergency phone numbers.'

I said, 'Da-ad!'

But he was way beyond communicating with; Dad was into chores like I was into Shakespeare. When he gets going, my father is so brisk and efficient that it can drive you nuts.

Just as I was considering patricide, Mum whisked me off to the supermarket.

Shopping for myself was different, but not so novel that I wanted to linger over it. So: Pizza, chill-and-heat meals . . .

'Salad!' said Mum. 'You mustn't forget to eat salad.'

. . . cheese, yoghurt, bread, mineral water.

Mum looked down into the trolley and frowned. 'Are you sure that'll be enough?'

'Yes.'

'It doesn't look much.'

'Mum, I won't starve. There are these places called takeaways . . .'

'You will take care of yourself, won't you?'

'No. I'm suddenly going to go round sticking my wet fingers into wall sockets.'

'Don't joke about it, Robert! I'm feeling guilty enough about leaving you as it is. Have I turned into one of those horrible career women who don't pay enough attention to their families?'

'No, just your regular neurotic, Mum.'

'Promise me you won't get drunk every night.'

'I promise! I also promise not to smoke crack or be butchered by a serial killer. Mum, this is Crossleigh, not New York. How much trouble do you think I can get myself into in a town like this?'

Massive close-up here: a still of my face with *Famous Last Words* printed underneath it.

At two o'clock I went round to Kev's house. He was in the bathroom when I arrived. His mum led me through into the kitchen and started talking to me in this low, urgent voice, like we were plotting an assassination attempt.

Mrs Ridell had the knack of wearing naff clothes – stuff like T-shirts printed in gold and black tiger-stripes – and looking classy in them. In fact, she was attractive enough for me to consider developing an older-woman thing for her, but that afternoon she was showing her age. Her face was pale and strained, like she hadn't been sleeping too well.

'Rob, is Kevin in trouble at school?'

'Not that I know of, Mrs R.'

'Only he's been acting strangely, not like his normal self. Have you noticed anything?'

I hadn't. Well, except for that one weird conversation. Getting it together with Milena had taken up all my attention. 'It's probably work pressure. We're all stressed. GCSE courses are pretty full-on.'

'I'm worried that it's more than that. I think it's . . .' Mrs Ridell shied away from whatever it was that she'd been going to say. 'Sons can find it difficult to talk to their mothers about . . . boy things. I think he misses his father but – well, you know.'

Actually I *did* know; it was what had made Kev and me bond. In Year Eight we'd been casual friends at school, seeing each other on Saturdays every once in a while. Then one Saturday, right out of nowhere, Kev told me about his parents getting a divorce and how screwed-up and betrayed he felt. It changed our relationship, because when someone tells you stuff like that you have to be on their side afterwards, right?

Mrs Ridell pleaded with her eyes. 'Would you talk to him?'

'Will do. Can't promise that it'll do any good, though.'

'It might. You know him better than I do. If anyone can get him to open up, it's you.'

The sound of a flushing toilet came from up-stairs, and we changed the subject but fast.

Kev was wearing his yellow hooded jacket, cement-coloured denim trousers with pilot-pockets and a pair of suede trainers with Velcro fastenings. He looked smart but hard: it was the kind of uniform a joy-rider who only broke into Jags and BMWs would wear.

So there we were, young and hot with Saturday

afternoon in front of us – and what did we do? We went down to the green.

Over the years, Kev and I had spent a lot of time at the green. It was where we'd tried smoking – how can anyone do that? – and lager, which had been great until the universe started spinning. We sat on a bench and I told Kev about my parents going away and leaving me behind.

Kev was impressed. 'So the world's your oyster.'

'Kev, have you *seen* what the inside of an oyster looks like?'

'You going to celebrate – like have a wild party?'

'Uh-uh! I'm on trust. One foot wrong, I get grounded until I'm thirty.'

'Up for a movie tonight?'

'Sorry, I thought it might be tactful to stay in with the folks, show them how quiet and responsible I am.'

'Tomorrow?'

'Er, actually I figured tomorrow would be a

good time for my date with Milena. But I could always . . .'

'Don't change your plans for me. It's cool.'

Kev sounded so sincere that I knew he didn't mean it.

'What gives with you, Kev?'

'How d'you mean?'

'Your mum says that you've been giving her a hard time.'

Kev groaned and rolled his eyes. 'Not you as well!'

'Not me as well what?'

'She keeps doing this thing where she grabs anyone who'll listen and talks about me behind my back. If she's got a problem, why doesn't she come out with it?'

'Because she doesn't think that she's the one with the problem.'

'Meaning it's down to me? Oh, cheers, Rob! I thought we were mates.'

'We are, and mates talk – so talk.'

Kev's crabbiness collapsed into depression. 'It's nothing. Mum's exaggerating.'

'You can't exaggerate nothing, Kev.'

'I've been sorting out some stuff, that's all.'

'About?'

'Me.'

'What kind of stuff?'

Kev twisted up his face, like he was finding words difficult. 'Ever feel your entire life is a lie, Rob? Nobody says who they really are, everything's fake and you just go along with it, pretend it's OK. You end up lying just like everybody else, because you're frightened someone's going to find out the truth.'

'Yeah, sure. I feel that way all the time.'

This was a downright lie and Kev spotted it right off. 'No you don't, Rob. You have no idea what I'm talking about, do you?'

'I might if you explained it to me.'

'You wouldn't.'

'How can you know I wouldn't?'

'Because I know, all right?'

We'd crossed Kev's border; the ground on the other side was swampy and I was stuck up to my waist.

'Just try me, Kev.'

'What's the point?'

'I'm your *friend* is the point!'

'I wouldn't be so sure about that. How can you be friends with someone when you don't know who they are?'

Kev's question gave me a jolt. He didn't know about Rosalind and no way was I going to tell him, but I'd never thought that there might be something Kev hadn't told me. 'Are you into drugs, Kev? Is that what this is all about?'

Kev laughed. 'I wish it was that easy! If I was on drugs at least I'd be getting something out of it.'

He stood up and looked at me, and I didn't

recognise his expression. 'I'm going to head back.'

I made to get up, but Kev said, 'Don't come with me, please? Leave me alone for a bit. Concentrate on Milena. I hope you both have a good time.'

He walked away.

'Kev? Kev!'

He didn't turn around.

Know that feeling you get when you think things are finally going your way? Don't trust it: it usually happens just before everything goes pear-shaped on you.

6

I'll put myself in poor and mean attire,
And with a kind of umber smirch my face

Mum and Dad left at eight o'clock. I got up to see
them off: Dad was a bit fussy and tearful; Mum
was quieter than usual, keeping her feelings in.
When the car was out of sight I felt a pang of
anxiety. If they'd turned around then and said
that they'd changed their minds about going

away, I would have been glad.

The house was emptier without them, less alive. I made myself a cup of instant coffee and sat in the lounge, slurping and thinking. I'd fulfilled a teen ambition: I had the house to myself and I could do what I liked, but there was a problem – what exactly was it that I'd like to do?

The first thing I decided was that I was going to listen to music instead of Radio Four – hey, Sunday morning without The Archers! I decided to investigate my parents' record collection. They had been born in the sixties, when rock and roll was the new rock and roll, and they'd collected a lot of vinyl; in fact, we're the only family I know that still owns a turntable. The usual suspects were there – The Beatles and The Rolling Stones – and a lot of stuff from the seventies, Mum's and Dad's teenage years. I pulled out some albums, laid them on the floor and looked at the pictures on the sleeves. The only one who looked like he really meant it was David

Bowie. On one of his album covers there was a painting of him as a man-dog, not quite animal, not quite human. The picture intrigued me, so I slipped the disc out of its sleeve, whapped it on the deck and let it rip.

It started with a jangly guitar riff that went round in a circle, like a peal of bells. The sound was raw, like any minute the backing group was going to fall apart, then Bowie started to sing and – lightning strike! – the song was about a boy–girl, or a girl–boy, all inclinations were catered for. I got that same feeling I'd had on stage on Friday, and all of a sudden Rosalind was back.

She cranked up the volume control and danced, grinding her hips, weaving the music together with her hands. Rosalind didn't care if anyone else thought she looked stupid, her dance went way beyond ridiculous; every movement was a statement of who she was, and if you didn't like it you could go do something biologically unpleasant to yourself. She used her body to tell stories, drop hints, make sly promises.

There was no line between Rosalind and me; we ran in and out of each other like the threads in a carpet. I'm going to put *I* for the next part, but I could put *Rosalind* or *Rosalind/I* and it would be the same.

I danced upstairs. Mum keeps this little zip-up bag in the airing cupboard. Inside the bag are bits of old make-up that she doesn't use any more but hasn't got the heart to throw away, and a little hand-mirror. I picked out a lipstick called Forbidden popped off the top and twisted the barrel until the point slid out: blood-red, shiny. I held the mirror in my left hand and wiped the tip of the lipstick across my mouth. It tasted greasy, like I'd just eaten a bacon sandwich. I felt guilty and excited: guilty because I felt excited, excited because I felt guilty. Next, eyeshadow. I rubbed my forefinger in tur-quoise stuff and smeared it over my lids. Then mascara, sweeping it on to my lashes the way I'd seen Mum do it, the brush tickling so much that it made me sneeze. My heart was thumping and I was quivering like I had a tuning-fork inside me. I turned to the mirror above the washbasin to see who I was.

This thing peered at me: overdone parody-tart; a male version of what a female ought to look like; a clown and, worst of all, a let-down. I wasn't a strong, independent, free female, just a guy with make-up on. Rosalind vanished in disgust and left Robert alone and humiliated.

I washed all the gunk off my face and scrubbed the basin with bathroom cleaner; then I went downstairs, put the records away and tuned in to Radio Four.

Dad rang. He said, 'We're at Heathrow. The flight's at ten. Everything all right?'

'Dad, you've only been gone forty-five minutes.

What can go wrong in forty-five minutes?'

'You never know.'

Had Dad picked up some sort of telepathic message that warned him that I'd been doing something I shouldn't? I don't think so; most probably it was just Dad being Dad. It would be nice if reality could be like The X-Files – you know, the family next door are aliens who want to steal your brain – but on the whole reality's not that interesting.

After the call from Dad, I made a Big Decision. I'd let Rosalind out of her box, put on make-up to try to look like her, and failed dismally, so that was going to be the end of it.

I should have known better. I should have seen that wanting to be someone else meant that I wasn't certain about my own identity, but I wasn't ready to confront that yet. It was easier to believe that I could shut Rosalind away and get on with my life – my conventional, straight, male life.

In fact, it was time to ring Milena.

* * *

I said, 'Hi, Milena! It's Robert.'

'You took your time. I thought you must have changed your mind.'

'I didn't want to rush things, you know?'

'Oh, why not?'

'I didn't want you to think I was desperate.'

Milena laughed. 'I *know* you're desperate, Robert. You don't have to play hard to get with me.'

'That's a relief! Are you doing anything this afternoon?'

'Yes, going out with you. That is why you rang, isn't it?'

Whoa! Sweet, shy Milena was also sharp, sarcastic and one step ahead.

I said, 'Where would you like to go?'

'Nowhere.'

'And what would you like to do when we get there?'

'Talk.'

'Is that all?'

Milena said, 'I want to be upfront about this, OK? You don't have to woo me, Robert. I'm not a chocolate-and-flowers sort of girl. Let's just hang for a while and see how it goes. You know the bus shelter on the green?'

'Yeah.'

'I'll be there about half-two. Is that all right with you?'

'Fine. I'll be there.'

'I know you will,' Milena said.

Sunday lunch is a ritual in my house. Because she's too busy to cook during the week, Mum makes up for it by insisting on doing a roast with all the trimmings, and we sit down together as a family and catch up with one another. That Sunday I lunched on pizza and it didn't taste the same as the pizzas you have when you're vegging out in front of the box. I missed Mum's roast potatoes; they were a lot more comforting than so-called comfort foods. After lunch I tidied the kitchen – and Dad would have been proud of me because I even wiped down the work surface – then I went to meet Milena.

Walking down the street, for the first time I noticed that it was spring. Leaves were budding on the trees, daffodils were nodding in the front gardens, the sunshine was warm but there was a chill edge to the breeze. I came over a bit corny about new beginnings and wondered if this might be a new beginning for me: the start of the journey that would lead to a job, marriage and children. I tried to picture myself really grown-up, say aged twenty-five, but I couldn't do it; it was too many years ahead.

I got to the bus shelter and found that Milena was already there. She was wearing faded jeans, a black top and a black leather biker-jacket with chrome studs. Her hair was tied back in a little bun. I'd had Milena pegged as ultra-feminine – floaty dresses in pastel colours – but instead she was tough cookie. People are often different inside and outside school; with Milena the contrast was startling.

She said, 'Hi!'

'Hi!'

And then there was an awkward silence.

Milena broke it by saying, *'Good morrow, fair Rosalind*! Why aren't you late? You were supposed to keep me waiting.'

'Was I? Sorry, I wasn't sure what I was supposed to do. This is my first date.'

'Mine too.'

'You're kidding!'

'No I'm not. Boys don't seem to like me.'

'I find that hard to believe.'

Milena hesitated, then said, 'Actually, that was the wrong way round. Boys used to scare me a lot. I could never imagine having a relationship with one. It was pretty worrying because I thought it meant that I preferred girls.'

How much nerve had it taken for her to say that?

Milena said, 'Are you shocked? Because if you've got a problem with it, we can forget the whole thing right now.'

'I'm not shocked.'

'So what are you?'

Good question: what was I, and what was that tingle shooting up my spine to freeze my scalp?

'Curious,' I said.

Milena chuckled at the back of her throat. 'I thought you would be. It's the same for you, isn't it? You don't know who to be.'

Did I gasp? I certainly felt like gasping. I said, 'How did you know that?'

'Because it's written all over you. Don't worry, not many people can read it. You have to've been there to spot it.'

Something passed between us, invisible lines of power crackling through the air.

I said, 'Can you feel that?'

'Uh-huh.'

'What is it?'

'Relief,' Milena said.

We went to Benton Country Park, which is a reclaimed gravel quarry. There's this big sign there with pictures of the birds that you're supposed to be able to see on the lake. The sign's always tickled me because it shows wading birds and the lake is about six metres deep like, have you ever seen a heron with six-metre long legs?

People were out in the sunshine, feeding bread to the mallard ducks and Canada geese; men in puke-coloured sweaters and tan slacks were knocking balls around the golf course; from the far side of the lake came the gentle splashing of windsurfers falling off their boards.

Milena said, 'Is it Robert, Bob or Bobby?'

'It's Rob. You?'

'Some of the girls in school call me Milly.'

'*Milly*? I don't think so.'

'Me neither. Milena will do.'

'It suits you. I'm not sure if my name suits me.'

'Well you can't go round calling yourself Rosalind – eyebrows would raise.'

I don't know why this was so funny – possibly because it was so close to the truth – but I had a hyena moment and giggled until tears ran down my face.

Milena tutted, said, 'Come here!' and started dabbing at my eyes with a tissue.

I said, 'What?'

'Your mascara's running.'

Was I embarrassed or what? I gabbled, 'God! Look, I don't wear make-up, right? It's just – my parents went to Amsterdam this morning, and I kind of wondered what I'd look like with make-up

on, so I – but it's the first time! I've never . . .!'

'No need to get defensive,' Milena said. 'I'm OK with it.' She put the tissue back in her pocket. 'And what did you look like?'

'A screaming queen.'

Milena regarded me critically, then shook her head. 'No, you're not a queen.'

'So what am I?'

'Well if you don't know, how am I supposed to? Let me guess, lots of eyeshadow and bright red lipstick, am I right?'

'You're not wrong.'

'Boys always go over the top when they put on make-up. They overcompensate because they want everybody to think that it's a joke. You ought to let me make you up sometime. I could find Rosalind for you.'

I ran my hand through my hair to keep the top of my head from popping off. 'This is crazy! I'm on my first date with a girl and we're discussing the finer points of make-up!'

'You'd prefer to pretend that we're normal?'

'It would be less confusing.'

Milena said, 'We don't know how long we're going to live, but we do know that we're going to be dead for ever. Confusion is all we've got time for.'

'I've never met anyone like you before.'

'Yes you have – you. We're sisters under the skin, Rob. Or is that brothers?'

I said, 'Who cares? It's us.'

We talked and talked. Most of it was confessional: attractions and turn-offs, fantasies that we hadn't admitted to anyone else. I hadn't realised how alike girls and boys are about stuff like that.

I said, 'When I was a kid, I used to love watching my mother get ready to go out. When she put on her make-up she went from being my mum to a movie star. And her clothes were smooth and silky.

I daydreamed about what it would feel like to wear clothes like that. Later, when I found out it was a no-no for boys to wear girls' clothes, I locked up the daydreams and threw away the key. Was it the same for you and boys?'

'No. I never wanted to wear boys' clothes. Boys frightened me. They were all shouting and stupid games I couldn't join in with. I felt safer around girls. Girls were more sensible. When I was in Year Eight, I got this massive crush on a girl in my form. If she didn't sit next to me in class, I'd be in floods of tears all day. She left school when her family moved to Devon. I thought it was the end of the world.'

'And since then?'

'No one.'

I was bewildered, exhilarated and terrified. Telling Milena about myself had been liberating, but maybe I'd said too much.

'Time to go,' said Milena.

'Shall I walk you home?'

'No. Shall I walk *you* home?'

'No. Am I going to see you tomorrow?'

'You want to?'

'Do you?'

Milena bumped me with her shoulder. 'Are we going to have an entire conversation in questions?'

'I've had enough questions. I'd like to find some answers. Tomorrow morning?'

'Now you're asking questions again.'

'OK, tomorrow morning, at the bus shelter, eleven o'clock. Let's get out of this dump and go somewhere happening.'

'Like where?'

'Like . . . Reading!' I said.

7

The sighing lover

I kept waking up through the night, wondering if I'd done the right thing, wondering what use Milena was going to make of what I'd told her. Eventually I calmed down enough to fall into a proper sleep and dreamed that the phone was ringing. It *was* ringing. I half-rolled, half-fell out of bed, staggered downstairs, racing the answering-machine, picked up the receiver and said, 'Hello?'

'Robert?'

'Well who else would it be, Dad? What's wrong?'

'Nothing. I just wondered how you were.'

'At seven forty-five in the morning?'

'Is it? It's an hour later here. We've just finished breakfast.'

'I'm happy for you.'

'Are you managing?'

'Yeah. Except for the fire.'

'What fire?'

'Relax, Dad! I'm winding you up. Everything's fine.'

Dad gave one of his sighs. 'Your mother's booked me on a barge trip around the city this morning.'

'Mind you don't get seasick.'

'How about you, what are you doing?'

'Er, standing in the hall, talking to you?'

Another sigh. 'I meant what are you going to do today?'

'Going into Reading with a friend.'

'Kevin?'

'No, another friend. Her name's Milena.'

'A girl?'

'Yes, a girl. Why d'you sound so surprised?'

'Because you haven't – you've never . . .'

'Well I am now.'

'What's she like?'

'A girl. Dad, I'm still in one piece and the house is still standing. Now get off the phone so that I can go back to bed. Love to Mum.'

'But . . .!'

'Say goodbye, Dad!'

'Goodbye, Dad.'

I grinned. I'd certainly given my parents something to think about. It was just as well that I'd misled them; I'd called Milena my friend, but as things turned out she was more like my accomplice.

* * *

Milena wore a short skirt, long sweater, thick tights, Doc Martens and a black PVC jacket with a matching handbag on a long strap. Her hair was down, and the way it flowed in the light made my throat constrict. I felt strange about her – she wasn't like the Milena in my English group, she wasn't the Milena I'd daydreamed about, so who was she? I was still trying to figure it out when she kissed me on the cheek.

'OK?' she said.

'Shellshocked. Did we really say all that stuff to each other yesterday?'

'Yup.'

'Weird!'

'Why?'

'You know Kevin Ridell? We've been best mates since we were in Year Eight, and I haven't told him half the things I told you.'

'Boys don't talk to other boys about things like

that. They're scared to admit that they have feelings. That's why they like playing contact sports, it's a chance to get physically close without emotional commitment.'

Milena smiled at me, and everything went so still that I thought it was about to rain.

I said, 'I didn't get a lot of sleep last night. I had an anxiety attack.'

'Why?'

'You. I never got so close to anyone so fast before.'

'And it bothers you?'

'Too right it does! If you told anybody else what I told you, you could mess up my life big-time.'

'I wouldn't do that, Rob.'

'Wouldn't you?'

Milena took my hand and gently squeezed it. 'We have to trust each other, Rob. Trust means taking risks, but if we don't, this is just a boy–girl thing.'

'What's so wrong with that?'

'Because I know we can be more. We can be extraordinary.'

'Like make our own rules and stuff what everybody else thinks?'

'Exactly.'

'Think we can?'

'Want to stick around and find out?'

I had the feeling that if I backed away from being extraordinary, I was going to lose Milena and I didn't want to. I had another feeling too: ever been on one of those fairground rides where you know you're going to be scared witless, and you are, but as soon as you get off you want to go on it again? It was like that.

I said, 'Would you mind telling me something?'

'What?'

'Why me?'

'Why you what?'

'Yesterday you said that you didn't like boys

because they frightened you – so what are we doing together?'

Milena shrugged. 'You're different. I don't feel threatened by you. There's a gentleness about you that's . . .'

'More like a girl?'

Milena didn't answer.

I thought – Is she here for Rob, or Rosalind?

The bus came before I could ask her and it was just as well, because I wasn't entirely convinced that I wanted to know the answer.

8

Love is merely a madness

Reading, the city that never sleeps. Below its towering skyscrapers the streets teem with people of all races, creeds and colours, moving in time to the pulse of excitement that throbs through the paving stones . . .

Well, not exactly, but if you put it next to

Crossleigh, Reading is LA.

We strolled along the pedestrian precinct in Broad Street and stopped to look in the window of a shoe shop.

I said, 'They're nice!'

'Which ones?'

'The gold strappy ones.'

'Honestly, Rob – you're such a tart! The black ones next to them are better. Lower heels, more comfortable.' Milena looked at me. 'What size d'you take?'

'Thirty-nine. I've got really small feet.'

'That's the same size as me. Got any money on you?'

'I'm loaded! My parents left me enough cash to put a dent in the National Debt, so I ...' I suddenly caught where Milena was headed. 'Oh, no! Definitely and absolutely not!'

Milena grabbed my arm and pulled at me. 'Dare!' she said.

Inside the shop I broke out in a cold sweat. 'They're staring at me!' I whispered. 'They know I've come in here to buy ladies' shoes!'

'No they don't. You won't have to try the shoes on, I'll do it for you. I'm just a girl who's taken her boyfriend with her to pick out a pair of new shoes, right?'

'If you say so.'

An assistant came over. 'May I help you?'

'I'd like to try on the black wedge-heeled shoes you have in the window.'

'They're very fashionable this season, aren't they?'

'I set my own fashion,' Milena said. 'Have you got them in thirty-nine?'

'I'll check for you.'

The assistant disappeared into the back of the shop.

I said, 'How could you do that?'

'What?'

'Talk to the assistant like that?'

'It's a girl thing. Men get nervous in shops. They let the assistant bully them into buying things they don't want. She's here for my convenience, not the other way round – get it?'

'Have you been on an assertiveness course or something?'

'I don't need to.'

She didn't, either. When Milena put on the shoes, stood up and took a few steps, she was like the model you can't take your eyes off when she sashays down the catwalk.

'What d'you think, Rob?'

'Um, yeah, nice.'

'Just nice – not wow, terrific?'

I wasn't looking at the shoes, I was looking at Milena's ankles. Guys have ankles like they've cut two potatoes in half and stuffed them down the sides of their socks, but Milena's ankles were slender.

'Elegant,' I said.

I left the shop thirty-seven quid lighter, and one pair of black wedge-heeled shoes heavier. I was doing sums in my head: I hadn't touched my clothing allowance since Christmas, so I could replace the money from my building society account. Of course, I wouldn't have to replace it all, because Mum and Dad would expect me to spend some of what they'd left, so if I took out twenty . . .

Milena said, 'Now, the market.'

'What for?'

'A skirt and top to go with the shoes.'

'*What*?'

Milena locked me into her eyes. 'Devilment' is kind of an old-fashioned way of putting what I saw in them, but nothing else comes close. She said, '*If there be truth in sight, you are my Rosalind.*'

'Act Five, Scene Four,' I said. 'Let's do it!'

You know that illicit kick you get when you're doing something your parents wouldn't approve of? I had it in Reading that morning, and the kick sent me rocketing up into the stratosphere. We bought a skirt and top, a pair of nearly-black tights and some make-up.

Halfway through a cheese and pickle sandwich in a snack bar in the old town hall, I groaned and said, 'Oh, God, what am I doing?'

'Enjoying yourself?'

'But I shouldn't be!'

'Why not?'

'Because it's . . . it's . . . wrong!'

Milena put down her salad roll and leaned closer to me across the table. 'What's so wrong with it, Rob? You're not hurting anybody. People who run away from who they really are screw themselves up. You have to learn to accept yourself.'

I gave it a go. The idea of dressing in the clothes I'd just bought made my heart thump and my palms sweat. I was going to access something that had always been in me, but I'd only recently discovered.

But what was it?

Milena and I went back to my place. I left her looking through the records in the lounge and took the shopping bags upstairs. I'd just stripped down to my shorts when I heard Lou Reed start to sing 'Walk on the Wild Side' – good choice, Milena.

First the tights. Whoever thought *they* were a good idea? It was like rolling sausage skins over my legs, and it took a lot of twisting around to get them comfortable. Then the top, the silky material cold against my chest; then the skirt, fumbling with the fastening; finally the heels – hoo, wobbly! I paced up and down to get used to them; even low heels pitch you forward like you're walking downhill. I'd promised not to look in a mirror until the transformation was complete, so I went down the stairs really, really carefully and into the lounge.

Milena's mouth opened slightly. She was:
BLINK! BLINK! BLINK!

I said, 'What's the matter?'

'Turn around.'

I turned, Milena looked at me and – is that how guys look at girls, like chest, bum, legs? Creepy!

I said, 'I look a mess, don't I? Lucky I left the tags on. I'll take it all back first thing tomorrow and . . .'

'You don't look a mess,' said Milena. 'Sit down, I'll do your make-up.'

Now being made-up by someone else is something I could *really* get into; Milena got so close to me that I could feel her breath on my face. I found the eyeliner pencil a bit uncomfortable, but when she brushed shadow on to my eyelids it was an incredible turn-on. She finished my eyes off with dark brown mascara, applied lipstick with a brush, made me blot my lips with a tissue, then stood back and stared at me. She said, 'I thought you might need foundation, but you don't.'

'How do I look?'

'Close your eyes and come with me.'

She led me out into the hall. I guessed we were going to the long wall-mirror next to the coat hooks. Milena swivelled me around and said, 'Open your eyes.'

Me, but not me: my eyes subtly larger, my mouth fuller; not me, but the feminine part of me risen to the surface – Rosalind.

Rosalind touched her hair and made it bounce. 'What d'you reckon?'

Milena's eyes were shimmering. She put her hands up to my face, kissed me tenderly and briefly on the lips, then kissed me not so tenderly and not so briefly.

I thought I was going to have a heart attack; I thought the universe was just the two of us, falling through nothing.

Milena broke the kiss and frowned. 'I'm sorry! I

shouldn't have done that, but I couldn't help it. You look so beautiful!'

'Don't be sorry.'

'I've spoiled it all, haven't I? I can't – I'm not – I won't do it again!'

I said, 'Not even if I ask you to?'

And we did it again.

We hugged each other tightly.

I said, 'What's happening to us?'

'I don't know.'

'My calves are beginning to cramp.'

'Then let me go.'

'I don't want to.'

'Good! I don't want you to.'

'Maybe I should go get changed,' I said.

'No, don't! Not yet.'

There was more kissing, and it was *intense*.

I didn't get changed until much later, just before Milena left. I walked her as far as the front gate and watched her until she reached the corner and turned to wave.

Letting Rosalind loose again had made Milena let something loose too. Rosalind had turned us upside down and inside out until we were scrambled.

9

Here shall he see no enemy

The first thing I thought about when I woke up was Milena. I remembered how amazing it felt to be with her. The memory made me smile, and that's when I noticed my mouth-cramp. My lips were stiff and aching because kissing Milena had exercised facial muscles I hadn't known were there.

I showered, dressed, went downstairs and picked up the post. There were two pieces of non-junk mail, an envelope addressed to me and a picture postcard showing views of Amsterdam. Inside the envelope was an invitation from Gary Middleton.

PARTY!!!

The place: Gary's house

The date: Wednesday

The time: 8 till late

The theme: Gender-bending. Boys dress as girls, girls dress as boys. Be as OTT as you DARE!

Penalty for non-attendance: MISSING OUT!!!

It seemed I wasn't the only person who'd been influenced by studying *As You Like It*.

The phone rang. It was Kev. He said, 'You round this morning?'

'More like thin and cylindrical.'

'I need to talk.'

'Go right ahead!'

'No, not on the phone. Can I come around?'

'Only if you've been knocked unconscious first.'

Kev sighed. 'Spare me the cracks, OK, Rob? This is serious.'

'What's wrong?'

'What's right?'

'That bad, huh?'

'No, it's worse.'

Kev sounded as if he needed me to be a friend, not a comedian.

I said, 'Give me a half-hour?'

'Right. See you.'

I put the phone down, shovelled some breakfast inside me, then I went to my room, hid my Rosalind outfit at the back of the wardrobe, checked my face in the mirror to make absolutely sure it was free of make-up and gave the hall a quick hoover, just in case there was any incriminating evidence there. I wasn't ashamed of getting dressed up, I just didn't want to land myself in a situation where I had to explain it to anybody.

Kev turned up on time. He seemed nervous and he didn't say anything as he slumped on to the sofa in the lounge.

I said, 'So what's the problem?'

'I've had it with lying, Rob. I can't do it any more.'

'Who have you been lying to?'

'Everybody, including myself. I tried hiding it and it screwed me up, so last night I made up my mind to be honest. I came out to my mum.'

'What d'you mean, you came out? Came out of where?'

Kev made unblinking eye-contact. 'I'm gay, Rob.'

'This is a put-on, right?'

'No, I'm gay.'

'But you can't be!'

'Why not?'

'Because . . . because . . .'

Because he was Kev, the guy who knew every homophobic joke going. '. . . you've always been against that kind of thing.'

'Can you think of a better way to cover up the truth, Rob?'

'You can't be sure about something like that! Plenty of guys our age go through a phase where . . .'

Kev shook his head. 'You don't get it, do you? I'm not saying I think I *might* be gay, I *know* I am. I've tried to stop it by thinking about girls, but girls don't do it for me.'

'Oh my God! You're not in love with me, are you, Kev?'

Kev doubled over. I thought he was having a seizure or something, but he was laughing. It was a full minute before he was able to sit up again. 'Sorry! It was just the idea of . . . !' He struggled to stop laughing. 'No, Rob, I'm not in love with you.

You're my mate and anyway, you're not my type.'

I was kind of offended and I sounded sniffy when I said, 'How come?'

'Because you're – I don't know – family. I've never thought of you as anything but a friend. You're so egotistical, you know that?'

'What d'you mean, egotistical?'

'I tell you I'm gay and you immediately assume I must fancy you. What makes you think you're so hot, Rob?'

I was thinking about Kev, working out what was going to have to change: nothing. I'd never been interested in Kev's sex life, and I wasn't about to start. He was like me with Milena: I'd trusted her, now he was trusting me. I could take off my Rosalind outfit and go back to being Rob, but Kev couldn't change the way he was.

Kev misunderstood my silence and said, 'Are you disgusted?'

'Why should I be disgusted?'

'Because I'm not natural.'

'Who is, Kev? How long have you known?'

'Since I was seven.'

'Why didn't you tell me before?'

'I was afraid of how you'd react.'

'After all we've been through?'

'I didn't know what to expect.'

'Kev, we've thrown up together. I was there for you that sports day when your shorts split. Why would I reject you?'

'Because I'm not like you.'

'You never have been. What's the difference now?'

'You know I'm gay now.'

I had to show Kev that I trusted him the same way that he trusted me, and because it seemed to be own-up time, I said, 'I know I make a lot of bad jokes when I ought to be serious, but I'm being serious now, Kev. You're not the only one with secrets. When I had to wear a dress to act that scene in English? I enjoyed it. I tried wearing women's clothes again and I *still* enjoyed it. So you're gay and I'm a transvestite.'

Kev started crying. Just for a sec I didn't know what to do, then I did what I'd done the day Kev cried when he told me his parents were splitting up. I sat down on the sofa next to him and put my arm round his shoulders.

After Kev was all cried out, I said, 'What happens now?'

'I've done the tough part, telling Mum and you. Now I have to face the kids at school.'

'How are you going to do that?'

'Come out gradually. You know, tell a few people, see how it goes.'

'It won't be easy.'

'I know.'

It won't be easy was right up there with the Greatest Understatements of All Time. Crossleigh Comp, like most other schools, had its fair share of pupils who found it difficult to accept those whose sexual orientation was different from their own. They called themselves queer bashers.

I said, 'Whatever happens, I'll still be your friend.'

'They'll say you're gay too.'

'Let 'em.'

'Don't you mind?'

'I probably will at the time, but I'll get over it.'

Kev looked awkward. 'Rob, I . . .'

'If this is going to turn into a speech about how grateful you are for my support, forget it! I'm doing what a mate's supposed to do.'

'Did you mean all that stuff about being a transvestite?'

'Yes, and if you go to Gary Middleton's party tomorrow night, I'll prove it. Did he send you an invitation?'

'Yeah, but I don't think I'll go.'

'You should. We'll go together.'

'What about Milena?'

'The three of us will go.'

'Does she know about the, er . . .?'

'She helps me with my make-up.'

Kev boggled a bit. 'Are you going to tell her about me?'

'Would you mind if I did?'

Kev took a deep breath. 'No, I'd like you to tell her. If I'm going to live the truth about myself, I have to start somewhere.'

I punched his arm. 'You've already started, Kev.'

All the time Kev was there I felt positive and confident, kind of *you and me against the world*! But when he left I hit a trough and panicked. Everything was changing too quickly.

I wondered if it was my fault: was there something in me that acted as a magnet for misfits? Was I *really* as accepting of Kev's gayness as I'd made out? We'd never discussed sex that much, so it had never been an issue between us, but was it going to be an issue in the future?

And behind all the little questions lurked the Big One: did all the Rosalind stuff mean that I might be gay too?

I wished that my parents were around: not to talk to, just to be there, so I could know that at least one part of my life was stable.

After lunch I met Milena on the green and told her about Kev. She didn't seem particularly surprised. She said, 'This is the part of our lives where we have to find out who we're going to be. That's why adolescence sucks, because nothing's definite yet.'

'Kev sounded pretty definite.'

'He's lucky. He doesn't have doubts any more.'

'Sure! He's only got to worry about name-calling and physical assault. Lucky old Kev!'

Milena gave me a knowing look. 'And what are *you* worried about?'

'Me? Do I look worried?'

'Yes.'

'I've been thinking about yesterday afternoon. Were you kissing Rob or Rosalind?'

Milena's face told me that I'd asked her an awkward question and she answered it slowly, as though thinking out loud. 'The Orlando in me was kissing the Rosalind in you . . . and the Milena in me was kissing Rob. Who were you when we were kissing?'

'Everybody I am,' I said. 'Are we deviants, or what?'

'No, we're explorers!' Milena linked her arm through mine and squeezed. 'You know when it snows, and you see a patch of snow that nobody's stepped in and you just have to walk through it so you can be the first one to leave a mark?'

'Yes.'

'That's what we're doing.'

'What, going where no one's gone before?'

'Yes.'

'Sounds like the beginning of Star Trek.'

Milena laughed. 'I'll boldly go, if you will!'

So I boldly went. I told Milena about Gary Middleton's party and she caught light. 'We have to be there! You can wear the clothes we bought yesterday and I'll borrow something off my dad.'

'Is it OK if Kev comes with us? I sort of promised that he could.'

'Fine. We can hold one another up if the going gets tough. Now, where did we leave off yesterday?'

We found a quiet corner in Benson Park and did some more research into kissing. It wasn't the same as the first time, not so total, and I couldn't work out whether it was because of Milena or me.

I said, 'Is this love, or lust?'

'How d'you tell?'

'I don't know.'

'Maybe it's part love, part lust.'

Milena was right on the money, because if you

take part of 'love' and put it with part of 'lust', you get 'lost'. That's what we were, and it didn't feel such a bad place to be.

Oh, and I found out I wasn't gay; I wasn't anything you could put a label on.

10

There was a pretty redness in his lip

Dad said, '–obert? it's Da–.'

'Dad? I can hardly hear you.'

'. . . can hear . . . fine . . .'

'Yes, I'm fine. Everything's fine, no need to worry.'

'I'll be . . . so I should . . . about . . .'

I said, 'You're breaking up. Call me later if . . .'

The line went dead; so much for the communications revolution.

I wasn't too concerned about Dad's call; I knew that if it was important he'd ring again or e-mail me. Anyway, I had a lot of other things to think about.

Normally, I'm not what you'd call a party animal, but I got keyed up about Gary's party, because I was going to do something dangerous: I was going to make a statement about my feminine side, my relationship with Milena and my friendship with Kev.

So how did I while away the hours? Housework. When I'd finished the house gleamed and I felt that I'd achieved something. Maybe I was more like Dad than I'd cared to admit.

At six thirty I took a shower, washed and dried my hair, put on my Rosalind clothes and lost my nerve.

* * *

Milena arrived, looking like she'd been dined on by vampires: black lips, face covered in deathly-white slap. She wore a dinner jacket, a frilly-fronted shirt with a white bow tie, trousers with shiny stripes down the seams and black patent leather shoes. I yanked her inside, slammed the door shut, leaned back against it and said, 'I can't go through with this!'

'Yes you can.'

'I *cannot* go to a party in these clothes! Everyone's going to know!'

'Know what?'

'That I mean it – that I'm serious!'

Typical, huh? Like there's this part of you that says: *I'm not the same as everybody else, I'm an individual . . . but please don't let anyone notice me!*

'Rob, nobody at the party is going to look like who they are. They'll be in costumes, playing roles – it's theatre!'

'But we'll have to walk there! Suppose any of the neighbours see me?'

'They'll all be watching TV.'

'But what if they're not? What if one of them looks out the window as we go past?'

'Then they'll see Orlando and Rosalind.'

'I'm still a bit nervous.'

'You think I wasn't nervous, walking here in these clothes?' Milena hooked her thumbs under the lapels of her jacket. 'This isn't just a disguise, it's armour. People may stare at you but they don't see you. You're hidden inside.'

'So . . . pretending to pretend is going to keep people from knowing that I'm not pretending?'

Milena put her arms round my neck, kissed me and said, 'Sweet Rosalind, you'll be the fairest maiden there. Now let's get your make-up on and meet the public.'

She made my eyes a little darker this time and used a little more lipstick on me – like showy, but not tarty. Then I took Milena's arm, stepped outside and – enter Rosalind.

It was dusk: not daylight, not dark; the shifting shadows altered the shapes of things. The pavement felt uneven beneath my shoes and I discovered that a skirt lets in draughts in places you're not used to if you wear trousers. Then Rosalind really went for it; she threw back her head and laughed at the sky.

Milena said, 'How are you feeling?'

'Free – and naughty! I haven't felt naughty for years.'

'Save it for me. I don't want to catch you coming on to anyone else.'

'As if I would!'

'You wouldn't, but Rosalind might.'

And I thought – Well, yeah! She might at that.

Kev was waiting at the corner of his street and at first I thought he must have got a wire crossed, because he was wearing an oatmeal-coloured sweater, pale grey drawstring trousers and canvas loafers. He stared hard at me. 'Jeez, Rob, you look convincing!'

'That's more than I can say for you, Kev. You're supposed to be dressed as a girl.'

Kev leaned closer and blinked so I could catch his glittery eyeshadow. 'I'm a Shakespearean gender-bender,' he said. 'I'm a boy being a girl being a boy.'

We walked arm-in-arm with me in the middle. I thought we were the most incredible people in the world, and that together we were invincible.

A blast of music nearly knocked me off my wedge heels as Gary's front door was opened by a hooker with long, straight, suicide-blonde hair. She wore a red satin corset trimmed with black lace, matching knickers, suspenders and fishnet stockings, three-inch spike-heeled shoes and a pink feather boa draped across her shoulders. Her make-up looked like she'd put it on with a shovel: silvery-blue shadow up to her eyebrows, thick false lashes, slippery scarlet mouth.

I thought – Hmm! She's certainly got all her goods laid out on the counter!

The hooker said, 'Hey, Robert! Looking gorgeous!' – *and it was Gary*!

I gulped and said, 'Um, you look stunning yourself, sweetie. Are you going to let me and my boyfriends in, or do we have to stand on the doorstep all night?'

Gary spread his arms wide. 'Come in, darlings! But don't kiss me hello, you'll smudge my lipstick.'

Gary's house was filled with creatures on the borders of gender. Gary wasn't the only guy in a corset, and Milena wasn't the only girl in a DJ. I needn't have worried about standing out, because I was severely underdressed. Gary's mother was wearing a boiler suit and a flat cap; his father had on a black, strappy number, but his beard spoiled the effect.

There was dancing in the lounge, nibbles and low-alcohol punch in the kitchen, and fresh air in the back garden. Milena and I danced. Rosalind was an exhibitionist on the dance floor, gyrating her hips, snaking her arms and hands like an Indian temple-dancer. Milena danced with her shoulders, leaning into me and pulling back.

I danced with Kev – not the first time we'd danced together at a party, but we hadn't done it out of choice before.

Kev said, 'Enjoying yourself?'

'You bet! How about you?'

'Yeah, it's better than I thought it would be. You seen Terry Adams?'

'No.'

'He's over by the door.'

I looked. 'That's *Terry*?'

'Cute, isn't he? The purple wig really suits him.'

Someone tapped me on the shoulder. I turned around and saw Jane Wallace. She'd come in a white suit with flared trousers and a red silk shirt. Her hair was combed up in a quiff and the gold medallion round her neck made her look like something out of a seventies disco.

Jane said, 'May I?'

'Why, thank you.'

We showed each other our moves. Jane was pretty good, but she couldn't fit in with Rosalind the way that Milena could.

Jane said, 'Seeing you in those clothes is quite a revelation, Robert. Tell me, do you find ambiguity at all erotic?'

'I might if I knew what it meant.'

'Does being in a room filled with people dressed in the clothes of the opposite sex make you horny?'

'It's intriguing. Like anything's possible.'

Jane smiled. 'Boys will be girls and girls will be boys!'

When I finished dancing with Jane, I found Milena and Kev deep in conversation and I was pleased that they seemed to be getting on so well. Then Kev drifted away and started to socialise: every time I caught sight of him he was drinking, chatting to someone or dancing, or all three at once. He was laughing too loudly for too long, and his eyes were flat-looking, but I figured that he was probably OK and that if he needed help he'd ask me for it.

Milena and I went into the back garden to cool down. A big nearly-full moon was up and its light made Milena's dark eyes shine silver. She said, 'I was right, Rosalind. You *are* the fairest maiden here. The other boys are trying too hard – you're a natural.'

'Or is that an unnatural?'

'I don't think it matters tonight.'

'I'm glad I came. Thanks for talking me through the jitters.'

'You didn't take much persuading. Thanks for being here with me.'

I knew that Milena wasn't just talking about the

party. I said, 'This might not be love yet, but it's going to be, isn't it?'

'It's called falling, Rob.'

Falling: nothing to hold on to, no way of being in control; you can make believe you're flying until the ground comes up to smash you.

Things go wonky on me here. I was drunk on Rosalind so I don't remember how it happened, but at one point I found myself alone in the kitchen with Gary. Gary was primping and preening, stroking his wig and flourishing his boa. He said, 'How d'you get your legs looking so smooth?'

'I don't do anything. The hairs on my legs are pale, so they don't show.'

'I use depilatory cream. Waxing is murder – especially round the bikini line! What d'you do about armpit-rash?'

'Excuse me?'

'When you shave under your armpits, don't you get a rash?'

'I don't shave my armpits.'

Gary cocked an eyebrow. 'Oh, so you go for the natural look? Very French! Is that Max Factor lipstick?'

'Revlon.'

'I have to use hypoallergenic lipstick or my mouth swells up. Trouble is, it's so expensive!'

I lowered my voice to confidential level and said, 'Gary, have you done this kind of thing before?'

'Couple of times, at fancy dress parties. Great, isn't it? Makes you feel kind of . . .'

'Different?'

'Special. There's nothing like women's clothes – I mean, men's clothes are so boring, aren't they?'

I knew exactly what Gary meant, but I didn't want him to know that I knew. I said, 'Er, I'd better find out where Milena's got to. See you, Gary!'

If I hadn't been wearing heels, I would have run.

* * *

Milena and I left the party at eleven, so that she wouldn't miss her curfew. She insisted on walking me home, saying that it wasn't safe for a girl to be out on her own at that time of night.

Kev followed us outside to say goodbye. He'd drunk enough punch for it to show in the way he talked. He blew kisses to Milena and me and said, 'You guys are the best!'

'Yeah, Kev,' I said. 'We're wonderful.'

'No, I mean it! We should swear an oath.'

'Like blood brothers?'

Kev waved the suggestion away and the movement made him stagger. 'Nah, forget brothers and sisters stuff! No males, no females – we'll be blood people.'

He held his hand out flat, palm upwards. I put my hand into his and Milena put her hand on top of mine.

'Blood people,' we said together.

We were joking, and deadly serious.

Milena and I walked on with our arms wrapped round each other, my head resting on her left shoulder.

'Kev's all right, isn't he?' I said.

'I don't know. Is he always that hyper?'

'Only at parties.'

'Don't you think he was overdoing it a bit? Maybe we should have taken him home with us.'

'He's enjoying himself – and if he'd come with us, I wouldn't have you to myself.'

We continued in silence until we reached my front gate.

'I don't want this to end,' I said. 'Can't we put the world on hold?'

'Sorry. My folks barbecue me if I'm not in by a quarter to twelve. That just about gives us time to . . .' Milena waggled her eyebrows. 'Know what I've been wanting to do all night?'

We kissed. Milena leaned me backwards in her arms – real old Hollywood stuff! – and the kiss got longer and warmer: galaxies collided; stars condensed out of gas clouds and ignited.

And then the front door of my house opened, and Dad stepped out. His mouth gaped and his eyes bulged. *'Robert?'*

11

**Not out of your apparel,
and yet out of your suit**

I heard the deep, slow tolling of funeral bells. My voice went up two octaves. 'Dad – what are you doing here?'

'I live here, Robert. Why are you acting so surprised? I told you I was coming home tonight.'

'You did?'

'Yes. I rang you this morning to confirm the details I put on the postcard.'

'Er, the postcard?'

'I sent you one. Didn't you get it?'

Something heavy sank from my stomach to my feet. 'Oh, *that* postcard! I sort of haven't quite got around to reading it yet.'

Dad looked me up and down. 'Forgive my asking this, Robert, but what the hell d'you think you're doing?'

'Milena and I have been to a party.'

'Milena?' said Dad. He frowned at her, then his face relaxed. 'Oh, so *you're* Milena! How d'you do?'

Milena said, 'Hello, Mr Hunt,' and she sounded like she was apologising for something. I glanced at her and she wouldn't meet my eyes.

I said, 'It was kind of a fancy dress party thing, you know? The girls dressed as boys and . . .'

'Thank you, Robert. I know what a fancy dress party is. Believe it or not we had them back in my day. I think you'd both better come inside, before you get arrested.'

Milena took a step backwards. 'I have to get home, or my parents will . . .' She wheeled around and walked away.

Something was very wrong and I had to find out what it was, but when I made a move to follow Milena, Dad said, 'Robert! Inside, now!' in his take-no-prisoners voice.

I followed Dad into the lounge. He was antsy; the left corner of his mouth kept twitching.

I said, 'How was Amsterdam?'

'Dutch. Robert, is there something that you'd like to tell me?'

'No – should there be?'

'Oh no, of course not! It's quite normal for fathers to come home and find that their sons have turned into daughters!'

'I told you, I dressed up for the party, Dad!

What's the matter, have you got some sort of problem with that?'

'Yes I do, as a matter of fact. We all have irrational prejudices, Robert, and I'm afraid that men in women's clothing is one of mine. Seeing you dressed like that came as . . . well, a shock. I was concerned about you.'

'Why?'

'When I looked out of the window just now and saw you and Milena kissing, I thought that you were a girl and she was a boy. Then, when I realised the girl was you, I thought . . . Let's just say I was relieved when the boy turned out to be Milena.'

Dad and I had never had one of those cosy little chats about the Facts of Life – Dad had left that to school and Mum. Every time sex came up, Dad got embarrassed and changed the subject. Now he'd been confronted with the fact that I was sexually active and it had rattled him.

I said, 'Why were you relieved?'

'Because . . .'

'You thought I was kissing a boy and you were afraid that I was gay?'

Dad blushed and tried to say something that came out as a croak.

'Why would that worry you, Dad? It would be more like my worry, wouldn't it?'

Dad shook his head. 'Robert, would you go upstairs and get changed, please? I find it difficult to talk to you when you're wearing those clothes.'

'How come, Dad? It's still me.'

Dad squared his shoulders, building himself up for the Big Speech. 'I know it's not easy being your age, Robert. You can lose your way and get confused about your . . . preferences.'

'Preferences? You mean there's a choice? I thought people were born the way they are.'

'Yes, but they still have control over how they express it, and . . .' Dad then talked to me like he was Dad. 'It's not easy being my age either. You didn't come with an instruction manual, you know. Your mother and I had to learn how to raise you and we made plenty of mistakes along the way. All we can hope is that we got it right more often than we got it wrong. I just want you to know that, whatever you want to do, whoever you decide to be, your mother and I will support you the best way we can.'

It didn't sound clichéd at all. It was Dad, offering me love with no conditions, like he always had – though I hadn't always been able to see it that way. I'd been: me, me, me, the one the world revolved around.

So, what do you do when your father tells it like it is? You come out with a lame joke, right?

I said, 'No need to worry, Dad. You and Mum have done a pretty good job. I'm a red-blooded heterosexual male.'

'Good. Now will you go and change so we can get back to normal?'

Normal: that word again. I was beginning to

suspect that people used it to mean so many different things that it didn't actually mean anything.

Next morning the sun was shining, the sky was
blue and there was no hint that it was the start of
one of the worst days of my life.

At eleven o'clock, I phoned Milena.

'What was with you last night? You rushed off
without saying goodbye.'

'Robert, there's something I have to tell you.'

'What?'

'I don't think we should see each other for a
while.'

'Why not?'

'Because of last night.'

'Last night was brilliant!'

'I don't think your father thought so. When
he saw us together, the look on your face was . . .
It was like he'd caught us doing something that
we shouldn't. It made me feel ashamed.'

'But . . .'

'Rob, I'm not sure that we're good for each other. The whole Rosalind thing seems to be . . .'

'Hang on! You're the one who said . . .'

'Saying and doing aren't the same. I can't help the way I feel. I need time.'

'Time for what?'

'For working out exactly who is doing what to whom.'

'I thought we were falling in love.'

'But who are we, Rob? Who are we falling in love with?'

'Us!'

'Are we? When I was walking home last night, I started to think that maybe we were both in love with Rosalind.'

'Look, Milena, let's talk about this! Meet me at the . . .'

'I can't. I'm going to London with my parents. Family thing.'

'When will you be back?'

I heard voices on Milena's end of the line. She said, 'I must go. I'll call you sometime, all right?'

It wasn't all right, but there wasn't any choice. I'd watched enough soap operas to know that 'I need time' translated as 'You're dumped'. I didn't want to be dumped and even more than that, I didn't want to be on my own, it was too scary.

I reached for the phone to call Milena back and it rang before I could pick it up. I hoped it would be Milena, but it wasn't.

'Hello, is that Robert?'

'Yes.'

'It's Kevin's mother.'

'Hello, Mrs R.'

'I thought you should know that Kevin had an accident last night and I had to take him to the hospital. He's fine now, but . . .'

'Where is he?'

'At home. He's upstairs, asleep.'

'What happened?'

Mrs Ridell gulped hard. 'He, er, made a mistake with some tablets. He swallowed a bottle of paracetamol.'

I dropped the phone and walked straight out of the front door; I didn't even stop to put on a jacket.

12

And do not seek to take your charge
upon you
To bear your griefs yourself, and
leave me out

When Mrs Ridell opened the door and saw me, she grabbed hold of me and burst into tears.

'Thank God you've come, Robert! I don't know what to do.'

I didn't know what to do either, I'd never been cried on by an adult before. Feeling incredibly stiff and awkward, I patted Mrs Ridell's back and said, 'Come on. I'll make you a cup of tea.'

In the kitchen, Mrs Ridell blew her nose loudly, then gulped at the mug of tea I handed her.

'Has Kevin told you that he's gay?' she asked.

'The day after he told you.'

'I guessed a long time ago. I never mentioned it because I didn't want to believe it was true. I thought that in time, if he met the right girl, he'd change, but . . .' She sniffed back tears.

'What happened last night, Mrs R?'

'He came back from the party. I've never seen him so upset. He was raving and crying – I could hardly make out what he was saying. I lost my temper with him. I told him to grow up, pull himself together and stop all the gay nonsense.'

'You said it was nonsense?'

'I'm not sure what I said. I was frightened for him, for what his future was going to be like. This is all my fault. I should have listened. If I'd been more understanding, perhaps . . .'

Milena had been right, Kev *had* overdone it at Gary's party. He'd been on the edge and I hadn't registered it because I'd been too wound up in Rosalind, too pleased with myself for accepting Kev's gayness – like *Hey, I'm Mr Mature; I'm cool with everything*! Sometimes you can be so up yourself that you miss what really matters.

'You're not the only one to blame, Mrs R. It's my fault too.'

'How could it be? You weren't here.'

'I know, and I should have been.'

I poured myself some tea to keep Mrs Ridell company; the tea didn't taste of anything and was hard to swallow.

I said, 'What now?'

'Kevin has to attend a course of counselling – the hospital's arranging it all. Other than that, I don't know.'

'D'you think he'll talk to me?'

'I wish you'd try, Robert. He'll listen to you. You're very important to him.'

I thought Mrs Ridell was hinting at something. 'We're not – I mean, we don't love each other or anything.'

Mrs Ridell smiled sadly. 'Yes you do, but not in the way that you mean.'

I tapped on the door of Kev's bedroom. 'Kev, you awake?'

No answer.

I eased the door open and stepped inside. The curtains were drawn; the sunshine coming through them cast this freaky green light on the walls.

'Kev?'

The lump in the middle of the duvet on Kev's bed twitched and Kev stuck out his head. He looked terrible.

'How you doing?'

'Ever had your stomach pumped, Rob?' Kev's

voice was hoarse, like he had a heavy cold.

'Can't say I have.'

'I don't recommend it. Sit down, will you? I can't stand it when you're taller than me.'

I perched myself on the end of the mattress. 'You want to talk?'

'No.'

'That's tough, because you're going to. Why did you do it?'

'There was nothing worth watching on TV and I got bored.'

'Cut it out, Kev! I want to know.'

'D'you promise to leave me alone if I tell you?'

'No.'

Kev lay back on his pillow and stared at the ceiling. 'I thought I was doing all right. After you and Milena left, I went back to the party and talked to Gary. We snuck a bottle of vodka out of his Dad's stash and spiked the punch. We all got ... not wrecked but – you know?'

'Like acting stupid seemed like a good idea?'

'Right. Terry Adams asked me for a dance. He was well into being a girl by then, wiggling around and talking in a squeaky voice. Someone put on a slow track and Terry started smooching ... and then he snogged me.'

'He *what*?'

'He snogged me. Everybody whistled and cheered. Hilarious, huh, a guy kissing a guy? They were all staring and laughing and they *knew*, Rob. I could see it in their eyes. The kids at school aren't ever going to take me for what I am. I'll be a freak show, like I was last night.'

'No you won't. Look, you had too much to drink and it made you paranoid. Most of the people at the party probably don't remember a thing about what happened.'

Kev ignored me: it was what I deserved for coming out with something so feeble.

'I couldn't stay, I was too humiliated. I ran

outside, and . . .' Kev's voice cracked. 'There was nowhere to go, Rob.'

'Why didn't you come and see me?'

'You were with Milena. I didn't think you'd want me round. I went home and tried to tell my mum about it, but she just had a go at me. I couldn't handle it. It was like I was alone and I was always going to be that way, no one was ever going to care about me.'

I was sorry for him and angry with him, and myself. I said, 'So you tried to top yourself to make people feel guilty?'

'Something like that.'

'Well it worked on me and your mum.'

'Sorry, Rob.'

'Me too.'

'For?'

'Being a lousy friend, pretending to understand when I didn't, leaving you at the party after Milena said you weren't OK. I don't know what you're going through, Kev. I have no idea what it feels like to be gay.'

'It feels like being human, only you get persecuted for it.'

'Yeah, but you don't have to believe that the people who persecute you are right.'

Kev's eyes flashed resentment. 'That's easy for you to say, Rob. You straights don't know that you're born. This is your world. Turn on TV, what d'you see? Boy meets girl, parents and children – even in the ads. Gays are only allowed if they tell jokes about themselves.'

'Us straights don't have it all our own way, Kev.'

'Don't you?'

'No. Just before your mum rang, Milena gave me the boot.'

I hadn't meant to break down, but I did, and it was Kev's turn to put his arm around my shoulders.

It didn't matter that Kev was gay and I was

straight. What we'd believed would drive us apart brought us closer together.

Next day it was Good Friday but there wasn't anything good about it. I woke up with a concrete block of misery pinning me to the bed. I said, 'Milena,' as though speaking her name out loud would help in some way.

Eventually I went downstairs. Dad was in the utility room, whistling. His chirpiness grated.

I said, 'How come you're so cheerful this morning?'

'I'm sorry, I didn't know it had been made illegal. I'm cheerful because your mother's coming home this evening. Are you coming with me to meet her at the airport?'

'I don't think so. I wouldn't want to spoil the joyful reunion.'

Dad looked at me through narrowed eyes. 'A-a-h!'

'A-a-h what?'

'You've got girl trouble.'

Oh, great! It was so obvious that even my *father* could see it.

'No,' I said. 'I've got lack-of-girl trouble.'

'Have you and Milena fallen out?'

'I think she's dumped me.'

'Is there another boy?'

'No.'

'Another girl?'

'Who, me or Milena?'

Dad rolled his eyes and sighed one of his Dad-sighs. 'Have you been seeing another girl behind Milena's back?'

Tough call: the truth was yes, I'd been seeing another girl – Rosalind – and it hadn't been behind Milena's back; but I took the simple way out and lied.

'No. Milena's not sure that we're right for each other.'

'Are you?'

'I guess.'

'Then convince her.'

Dad made it sound so simple that I groaned.

'Stop being negative, Robert! Do something to show her that you care! Send her flowers, sweep her off her feet!'

'We don't do romantic, Dad. Milena's not into all that stuff. It wouldn't work.'

'Faint heart never won fair lady.'

I scowled. 'Is that a quote from Shakespeare?'

'It's a proverb – why, does it matter?'

'Yes. That guy Shakespeare has got a lot to answer for!'

'What's Shakespeare got to do with it?'

'Everything! If it hadn't been for him, I would never have . . .'

Dad held up his hand. 'Don't go on, please! You've got me confused. I can deal with confused, but totally bewildered would be beyond me. Just let me go on looking forward to seeing your mother and leave me in peace!'

The rest of the day was a blank. If you picture me hanging around the house, waiting for a phone call that didn't come, you've pretty much got it.

Mum and Dad got back from the airport at nine. Mum looked concerned. She gave me a hug and said, 'How's my favourite son?'

'So-so.'

'What's all this your father's been telling me about you and Milena?'

'It depends on what he's been telling you.'

'That you've had a row with her.'

'Not exactly.'

'Pity. You could've kissed and made up. Would it help to talk to me about it?'

'It's complicated.'

'I can manage complicated.'

I appreciated Mum's wanting to help, but I

couldn't think of a way to tell her what was wrong. I gave her a flimsy smile and said, 'Thanks for the offer. I might take you up on it sometime.'

Mum pursed her lips, mock-offended. 'I was going to give you the present I bought you in Amsterdam, but since you refuse the benefit of my motherly wisdom, I don't think I'll bother.'

'What present?'

Mum handed me a carrier bag that contained a large box. I took out the box, shook it and it rattled. 'What's this?'

'Oh, fruit-flavoured condoms, a pair of nipple clamps, a packet of chocolate willies . . .'

'Mu-um!'

'Open it and see.'

So I opened it, and saw. Mum had bought me a pair of calf-length cowboy boots – tooled leather, chisel toes and high heels. Like, high heels for men.

I didn't know whether to laugh or cry.

13

O my poor Rosalind,

wither wilt thou go?

Kev and I spent a lot of time together that holiday, working on getting his self-esteem back. I made him write out a list of the kids at school whose opinion mattered to him, and another list of the kids he couldn't care less about. There were six names on the first list; the second ran to two sides of A4.

'There you go!' I said. 'You're not as worried about what other people think of you as you thought. Paranoia's an ego-trip.'

Kev gave me a doubtful look. 'It is?'

'Yeah! It's like you believe you're so important that everybody else has got nothing better to do than gossip about you – and I should know.'

I gave Kev the uncut version of Rob, Rosalind and Milena; he gave me some insight into what it was like to be gay in a straight world. Talking took my mind off the pain. Sometimes it was a background ache, other times it was so sharp that I could barely function.

One afternoon when I was so down you needed scuba gear to get to me, Kev said, 'I don't understand Milena's problem. If she was so keen on helping you to be Rosalind, why did she back off?'

'Search me.'

'Why don't you ask her?'

'How?'

'Pick up a phone.'

'It's not a phone thing, Kev.'

'Go see her.'

'I can't.'

'Why not?'

'She has to make the first move because she's the one with the problem. If I try to force things, I might screw up. Besides, it would make me look pathetic.'

'But, Rob, you *are* pathetic!'

The truth was, I was. I was also scared, and as the start of term got closer the fear grew until it was all I could think about.

When I went back to school I avoided Milena as much as possible. As long as she didn't tell me it was over face to face, there was still hope. On the way to and from school I continually bleated the same message to Kev.

'Milena didn't talk to me today.'

'That's tough.'

'No, that's good. It means she hasn't made up her mind yet. She's still thinking it over. If she really wanted to finish with me, she'd come right out with it, wouldn't she?'

'Would she?'

'Sure she would, and she hasn't, so I must still be in with a chance.'

I thought it made sense. I thought I was thinking clearly, when in fact I was lost in a maze, and even though I'd built it myself I had no idea of the way out.

Tuesday afternoon, I took a holiday from my own problems and thought about somebody else for a change.

It was at the end of school. I was walking down a corridor, thinking about Milena – what else? – when Gary Middleton came up to me and said, 'Rob, are you still hanging out with Kev Ridell?'

'Sure.'

'Didn't you hear about him and Terry at my party?'

'Yes. Kev told me about it.'

'What did he say?'

'The words "your business" and "none of" spring to mind, Gary. Why d'you want to know?'

Gary's eyes were shifty. 'Terry was just having a laugh, you know? But Kevin was like he meant it. I reckon he's bit . . .' He fluttered his eyelashes, pursed his lips and wiggled his hips.

'You mean he's gay?'

'Um, yeah.'

'So what if he is?'

'Well . . . you know.'

'No I don't!'

'I just thought someone ought to warn you.'

'Thanks for the concern, but I don't need to be warned. Kev and I are mates, and we're going to carry on being mates no matter what you or anyone else thinks. If you've got any objections, I suggest you stick them where the sun doesn't shine.'

Gary looked like he wanted to walk away, but something kept him there. 'Has he ever . . .?'

'What?'

'Like, tried anything on with you?'

'What's the matter, Gary – jealous?'

Gary blushed. He tried to say something, but all that came out was a croak.

I felt sorry for the guy: he had a lot of issues that he hadn't confronted yet. In the end, I was the one who walked away. I had to, because I was starting to enjoy watching Gary squirm and I was ashamed of myself.

Kev had been incredibly patient with me, but on Thursday the first thing he said was, 'Remember how you told me we'd be friends no matter what I did?'

'What did you do?'

'I rang Milena last night.'

'Huh?'

'I told her she has to talk to you.'

'Kev, you . . . ! What did you do that for?'

'Because you can't go on like this, Rob. If you were an animal, a vet would have put you out of your misery ages ago.'

'What misery? I'm all right.'

'No you're not. I've done you a favour, Rob. Milena will be waiting for you in the library after school, and you're going to be there.'

I stopped being annoyed with Kev; he was trying to put things right between me and Milena because he couldn't put things right for himself.

'OK, I'll go to the library. But what do I do if she tells me she doesn't want to see me again?'

'You start getting over it.'

I wasn't so sure that I wanted to get over it. Misery was better than nothing.

* * *

The schoolday was unreal; there was a plate-glass screen between me and the world. I kept inventing ways of getting out of talking to Milena. For about fifteen seconds I gave optimism a whirl and tried to convince myself that Milena was going to fall into my arms, but my sense of doom was too strong.

Last lesson ended. I waited for the home time scrum to disperse, then trudged up to the library.

Milena was waiting at one of the tables in the reference section. Her face was pale and serious and she didn't smile when I sat down opposite her. It was like being with a stranger.

I said, 'I need to know what's going on.'

'Nothing's going on.'

Milena's voice was flat and didn't give anything away.

'Are we still an item?'

'No.'

I thought I was going to throw up. 'What did I do wrong, Milena?'

'It isn't what you did, it's what *we* did. We should never have got into the Rosalind thing.'

'But you were as excited about it as I was.'

'It was OK while it was a game between the two of us – but when your dad saw us, I felt guilty.'

'Why?'

'We never thought about where we were heading, Rob. I got so caught up in your fantasy, I didn't see that you were using me.'

'I wasn't!'

'Not deliberately, maybe, but I felt used all the same. I can't lose that feeling, and I can't compete with Rosalind. I won't settle for being the second-best girl in anyone's life.'

'You're the *only* girl in my life.'

'We both know that's not true.'

I didn't have any pride left. I said, 'I'm sorry. I never meant to make you feel used or guilty. It's my fault. Tell me what I can do to make it up to you.'

'You can't make it up to me, Rob. It's us. When we're together it's . . . unhealthy.'

'Then why does it feel so good?'

'It doesn't any more.'

'We can . . .'

'No we can't. Let it go, Rob. Forget it ever happened.'

Cue: Milena standing up and walking out of the library; me sitting staring at where she'd been. The Rosalind game had started off as innocent, but the innocence had somehow got lost and there was no way to get it back.

I went to see Kev. He listened to me whine on about Milena and when I finally finished he said, 'And that's it – you're going to leave things like that?'

'What else can I do? She feels guilty when we're

together, what am I supposed to do?'

'You have to think of something. You found someone special, Rob, d'you know how lucky that is? I wish I could find someone. I might have to wait years before Mr Right comes along. Isn't Milena worth fighting for?'

'Not if she's the one I have to fight.'

'Come on, Rob! Don't just lie there like a stranded jellyfish waiting for the sun to dry you out – do something!'

'I can't think of anything that wouldn't make things worse.'

Kev laughed. 'Things could be worse?'

It was down to me again. I was afraid that I'd told Milena too much about myself, but I hadn't told her enough. There was more to me than Rosalind, but I hadn't let her see it because Rosalind was more important to me than Milena. I hadn't been fair to either of them. I'd treated Rosalind like she was separate from me, a different person, and it wasn't true; I wasn't two people, I was just me.

I had a lot of amends to make, especially to Milena.

14

Exits

Friday night was Moody Teen night. When I said anything to my parents, which wasn't often, it was in grunts. I kept thinking that I ought to be with Milena, doing the things that other couples did on Friday night – like snogging at the movies, sharing a pizza and having a conversation about the erotic possibilities of melted cheese. Instead I was stuck in with Mum and Dad, watching Gardener's World.

Mum had been giving me sideways glances all evening, trying to make contact, and I'd been ignoring her, but just as Alan Titchmarsh was turning over his compost heap, Mum tapped me on the knee and said, 'Get your coat.'

'My coat?'

'We're going to exercise the dog.'

I thought Mum had flipped. 'But we don't have a dog.'

'Then we'll just have to go for a walk by ourselves, won't we? It's time for us to have that talk we didn't have last week.'

I heaved a big, nobody-understands sigh and did as I was told.

We walked along the street, in and out of the splashes of lamplight on the pavement.

Mum said, 'Tell me about Milena.'

'Why?'

'Because I want to interfere with your private life.'

Mum wasn't going to leave it, so I caved in. 'She's beautiful, wonderful, bright, funny and she doesn't want to go out with me any more.'

'Why not?'

'I don't know.'

'Rubbish! You know perfectly well, that's why you're moping about the place. What went wrong? Forget I'm your mother, treat me as though I'm . . .'

'A friend?'

Mum shuddered. 'Perish the thought! I know mothers who try to be friends with their teenage children, and they're ghastly! Pretend I'm a total stranger, someone you can say anything to.'

I gave it a shot. 'OK, basically the problem is that Milena and I got off on the wrong foot. I pretended to be someone I'm not, she saw through me and now she thinks that I was dishonest with her.'

I don't think even *I* could have sorted the truth from the lies in that little lot.

'Were you trying to impress her?' Mum said.

'Something like that.'

'If you weren't being you, how are you going to show her who you are?'

'I'm not sure I can. I've been considering a change of image, you know? Finding my own style.'

Mum thought for a moment. 'Careful, Robert. A change of image doesn't always mean a change of heart.'

'I know, and it isn't as simple as I made out. See, the person I was pretending to be *was* me – a part of me, anyway. I let Milena think that the part was the whole thing. Now I have to put the part back so the join doesn't show and ... Is any of this making sense?'

'Not a lot,' said Mum. 'But it reminds me of something.'

'What?'

'Your father and I. I had trouble with him when we first met.'

'Did you?'

'I knew that we'd fallen in love with each other at first sight, but it took me a long time to convince him. He was so shy – no confidence at all.'

'How did you get round it?'

Mum told me.

I laughed and said, 'You did *what*?'

Mum told me again.

I said, 'That's the most devious thing I ever heard!'

'I can be devious if I have to be, Robert. How d'you think I got to run my own company? Anyway, the point is, devious or not, it worked. If it hadn't you wouldn't have been born, so be grateful.'

'Are you saying that if it worked for you and

Dad, it might work for me and Milena?'

Mum pulled an innocent face. 'I'm not saying anything. It's your life.'

And so it was, and by the time we got home I had a plan that I hoped would make it a whole lot better.

Saturday morning I was the first one up. I made a pot of coffee and some toast and had breakfast in the kitchen, flicking through the Yellow Pages.

Dad appeared, blinking like a tortoise. 'You're up early!' he said.

'Things to do.'

'Such as?'

'I'm going to Milena's house this afternoon. You know that single-breasted linen jacket of yours, can I borrow it?'

Dad's blink rate accelerated. 'Sure, I'll get it out for you. What are you looking up in the Yellow Pages?'

'Hairdressers.'

Dad stopped blinking and stared. 'Don't tell me you're thinking of having your hair dyed dayglo orange!'

'No, I'm going to have it cut.'

'A haircut? It must be love!'

'Yeah, love, friendship, whatever. I'm not fussed.'

Dad looked regretful. 'So, it's come at last! I knew it had to happen one day, but I wasn't expecting it to be quite so soon.'

'What are you on about, Dad?'

'You're starting to mature.'

'Because I'm having my hair cut?'

'Because of *why* you're having your hair cut.'

When your parents say something that shows they understand you, it can be irritating, but this time I didn't mind. I said, 'What is maturity, anyway?'

'Beats me, Robert. If I ever get to it, I'll let you know.'

I managed to get an eleven o'clock appointment at a place called Snippers which was – wouldn't you know it? – a unisex salon. Mum and Dad left for the supermarket and I went back to my bedroom to try on my boots. They were stiff and unfriendly, but I could walk in them; all the practice I'd had in wedge-heeled shoes paid off. I stuck plasters over the parts of my feet where the boots were most likely to rub blisters, put on a pair of thicker socks and I was ready to roll.

When it comes to boredom, having your hair cut is right up there with cookery programmes and televised award ceremonies. All you can do is sit while the hairdresser cuts off bits of you and blitzes you with small talk that's so small you need a magnifying glass to follow it. I endured it as patiently as I could, and when the hairdresser let me look at myself in the mirror – Bingo! The new Robert Hunt; or at least, Robert Hunt with a new hairdo.

* * *

Getting ready took time, but at last I was happy with it: crisp white shirt, thin black tie, grey-beige chinos, Dad's linen jacket, a drover's coat and my new boots. We were talking gunslinger; we were talking John Wayne and Clint Eastwood; we were talking *smell my pheromones*!

When my parents saw me, Mum did a double-take. 'My God, Robert! You look ... you look ...'

I said, 'Yes, I do, don't I?'

Dad walked up to me, slapped me on the back and said, 'Go get her, son!' like I was supposed to bring Milena home slung over my shoulder or something.

Optimism has a nasty habit of running out on you just when you need it most. On my way to Milena's doubts began to emerge, but I knew that I couldn't go back; I owed it to Milena.

I paused outside her house. The front path

seemed to stretch as I looked at it, or maybe I was shrinking. The windows stared at me like hostile eyes that said, 'We don't take kindly to strangers round these parts, mister!'

Mrs Griffin opened the door. Her hair and eyes were the same colour as Milena's.

'Yes?'

'Good afternoon, Mrs Griffin. I'm Robert Hunt, a friend of Milena's. We're in the same English group at school.'

'Oh, I am sorry! Milena is not here. She has gone shopping. She will be back soon.' Mrs Griffin had a faint accent and her grammar was textbook-precise.

'That's all right. Actually, it was you and your husband that I wanted to see.'

Mrs Griffin showed me into the lounge. Mr Griffin was sitting on a sofa, reading a newspaper. He stood up when I entered, and there was a lot of him to stand – he was over two metres tall, with shoulders like an American football player.

Mrs Griffin introduced us and Mr Griffin shook my hand. 'Sit down, Robert,' he said. 'What can we do for you?' He sounded friendly, but he was obviously puzzled.

This was my big moment and I had to give the performance of a lifetime. 'I'd like to invite Milena out this evening to see a film . . .'

Notice I said 'film'? Do I know how to communicate with the older generation or what?

'. . . and I've come to ask your permission.'

'Permission?' said Mr Griffin.

'Yes. I couldn't possibly ask Milena out if you had any objections.'

Mr Griffin frowned, smiled, raised his hands and let them drop. 'This is a bit, um, old-fashioned, isn't it?'

'I don't think that good manners ever go out of fashion, do they, Mr Griffin? If Milena accepts my invitation, I'll make sure she gets home safely and on time. I know how my parents worry if I'm home late.'

Mrs Griffin gazed at me like I was a vision. 'But this is charming! You are so proper, Robert. Yes, ask Milena out and if she says no, please ask me!'

We all laughed and it snapped the tension. Mrs Griffin made me a cup of tea and Mr Griffin and I talked about football, as guys do when they're trying to get to know each other. When football was exhausted, I asked Mrs Griffin about the Czech Republic.

By the time Milena got back, I had her parents on-side. It was three against one; she didn't stand a chance.

Milena walked me to the front gate. She was fuming like a traction engine. 'You stitched me up! I can't believe that you'd do that!'

'Believe!'

'Of all the sneaky, underhand . . .'

'Whatever it takes.'

'I've never been so embarrassed in . . .!'

I said, 'I miss you.'

It stopped her, but not for long. 'Oh, yeah, right, go on – add emotional blackmail to the list!'

'Tell me you haven't missed me and I'll walk away.'

Silence.

'Milena, you don't have to come out with me if you don't want to.'

'After the stunt you just pulled? My mother thinks the sun shines out of your backside! If I turned you down now, I'd never hear the end of it. It'd be "Milena, Milena! How could you be so cruel to such a nice young man?" Hah!'

Milena was running out of steam, more sulky than seething.

I said, 'No more girls' clothing, no more make-up. I'm the boy and you're the girl, right?'

Grudgingly, Milena said, 'I like your hair.'

'Good, I did it for you. It cost me an arm and a leg and you're worth it.'

'Those boots are . . .'

'Sexy? Yeah, I know.'

'Is that your jacket?'

'It's my dad's. I thought this time I'd dress as a male.'

'No more Rosalind?'

'No.'

Milena teased me with her eyes. 'Not ever?'

It's difficult to describe how this made me feel, but if you let a piece of meringue dissolve on your tongue, you'll get the idea.

'Rosalind's still here, Milena. She's me. I don't need a costume to be her. I mean, take away our clothes and what have you got?'

'Indecent exposure?'

'You've got a boy and a girl – basic fact that can't be changed without expensive surgery. The rest is open to negotiation. Clothes don't make us what we are, we do!'

Milena reached out, held my face in her hands and kissed me – just like our first kiss.

I said, 'What was that for?'

'I couldn't help it,' said Milena. 'You look so beautiful.'

Think that's it? Like, end of complications, everything neatly packaged with a ribbonbow on top? Get out more! This was the beginning of my first serious relationship, and if you think love doesn't include hurt, misunderstanding, rows over nothing and pointless jealousy, you just haven't been there. Sure, it can also be wonderful, exhilarating and magical, but I wouldn't want to give you a false impression. As Shakespeare said, *The course of true love never did run smooth*.

All this happened a year ago, so now we're in Year Eleven and the long shadow of GCSE exams has fallen over everything. Milena and I are still together. I don't know if we're the Great Love of each other's lives, but we're not bored yet. And don't bother to ask if I ever dressed up as Rosalind for Milena again, because I'm not about to tell you.

Kev's hanging on in there, waiting for Mr Right. Just about all our year knows that he's gay now; not everybody's happy with it, but he hasn't had his head kicked in so far.

Weird, isn't it? Sex is everywhere you look: in magazines and books, on TV and in the movies; advertisers use it to sell everything from cars to ice cream. The media feature sex so often, you'd figure that by now people would know pretty much all there is to know. But when you get right down to it, sex is something that gives people grief because somewhere along the line it got mixed up with what's right and wrong, what's good and bad. Maybe sex is evolution's practical joke on the human race.

I'm going to leave you with this thought: gay, straight, both, neither, any way you cut it you're in for a bumpy ride. Hold on tight and whatever you do, don't lose yourself, because you're all that you've got.

Take care – and good luck!

If you enjoyed this book, try some more fantastic
teen titles from Mammoth

Falling into Glory

Robert Westall

Seventeen-year-old Robbie has brilliant
exam results and a history of triumphs on
the rugby field – until he develops a close
relationship with a teacher, Emma Harris.
For Robbie, school, sport, and his family
begin to lose their importance – but what
does Emma want? Is she prepared to risk
her whole career for him?

Together they take an Icarus flight almost
too near the sun.

Love Match

Robert Westall

Making the wrong choice, falling in love at the wrong time, loving the unattainable . . .

Love Match is a thought-provoking collection of stories which conveys the drama, pain and joy of falling in love.

Points North

An anthology of Scottish writing by

Julie Bertagna, Theresa Breslin, Chris Dolan,

Lindsey Fraser, Jackie Kay, Gordon Legge,

Candia McWilliam, Dilys Rose

and Iain Crichton Smith, ed. Lindsey Fraser

Dark secrets, sticky jam, old clothes and

love-struck zombies . . .

Parents become friends; friends become

enemies . . .

Time passes and experience tells.

No ordinary stories from Scotland's finest writers.

Flame Angels

An anthology of Irish writing by

Dermot Bolger, Herbie Brennan, June Considine,

John McGahern, Marilyn McLaughlin,

Joseph O'Conner, David O'Doherty and

Michael Tubridy, ed. Polly Nolan

Freak?

Flower child?

True believer?

Who are you?

Coming home?

Climbing mountains?

Where are you going?

Some of Ireland's best writers tell how the
smallest thing can change your life, for ever.

Mary Wolf

Cynthia D Grant

When Mary's father loses his job, life
changes for the whole family. As the weeks
turn into months, Mr Wolf becomes even more
volatile and a catastrophe seems almost
inevitable . . .

What happens when you're the only one
who can see what's happening? Is there
anyone you can turn to when your life
has changed beyond recognition?

Uncle Vampire

Cynthia D Grant

Carolyn is desperate to reveal the secret of her uncle's awful night visits to someone – her older sister, Maggie, maybe, or her parents. But she is sure they'll think she's crazy and besides, her popular twin sister Honey thinks they should keep quiet.

But what if Uncle Toddy is a vampire? Carolyn is being drained . . . he could even turn her into a vampire. But here is a way to get rid of the vampire – drag him into the light.

Shadow Man

Cynthia D Grant

Gabe McCloud is just eighteen when he dies in
a car crash. Gabe was drunk at the time and his
death is seen as almost inevitable by some –
what could be expected from someone in his
family – an alcoholic and abusive father; a
mother poisoned by hatred, and a brother
who takes after the father . . .?

But for others – his girlfriend Jennie, his teacher
Carolyn, his friend Donald, Gabe's
life, and death, casts a shadow over their
lives and no one will ever be quite
the same.

The White Horse

Cynthia D Grant

Her mother's eyes glittered, always the sign that the fuse had been lit. The other kids would hide while the one she hit cried.

Raina is sixteen. Thrown out by her junkie mother, the only person who she can reach is her class teacher, and then only through her writing. Ms Johnson doesn't know how to help this insolent, aggressive girl. Yet it seems as if she's Raina's last hope.

When there's nowhere else to turn, can the teacher save her?